Victor-Lévy Beaulieu

Critic and polemicist, Victor-Lévy Beaulieu has published articles in almost every newspaper in Quebec, notably *Le Devoir*. Beaulieu, who once lived in Saint-Jean-de-Dieu, the setting for *The Grandfathers*, never completed his post-secondary studies, working instead in a bank and then as a secretary to a script writer. For five years he was Editions du Jour's literary director, finally leaving to found his own publishing house, L'Aurore. In addition, he teaches at Université du Québec and is a dedicated reader of both French and English classics. To date he has written eight novels, three book-length essays, and two of his plays have been produced on stage. *Les Grands-pères*, awarded the GRAND PRIX LITTÉRAIRE of Montreal in 1972, and *Jack Kérouac*, "the first liberated novel of the future" according to Claude Mauriac, have been published in Paris.

THE "FRENCH WRITERS OF CANADA" SERIES

The purpose of this series is to bring to English readers, for the first time, in a uniform and inexpensive format, a selection of outstanding and representative works of fiction by French authors in Canada. Individual titles in the series will range from the most modern work to the classic. Our editors have examined the entire repertory of French fiction in this country to ensure that each book that is selected will reflect important literary and social trends, in addition to having evident aesthetic value.

Current Titles in the Series

Ethel and the Terrorist, a novel by Claude Jasmin, translated by David Walker.

The Temple on the River, a novel by Jacques Hébert, translated by Gerald Taaffe.

Ashini, a novel by Yves Thériault, translated by Gwendolyn Moore.

N'Tsuk, a novel by Yves Thériault, translated by Gwendolyn Moore.

(continued inside back cover)

The Grandfathers

a novel by
Victor-Lévy Beaulieu

translated by
Marc Plourde

Advisory Editors

Ben-Zion Shek,
Department of French,
University of Toronto.

Réjean Robidoux,
Département d'Études Françaises,
University of Ottawa.

Copyright © 1974, 1975 by Harvest House Ltd.
All rights reserved.
ISBN 88772 160 5
Deposited in the Bibliothèque Nationale
of Quebec
1st quarter, 1975.
Originally published in the French language
by les Éditions du Jour, Montreal,
as *Les Grands-pères*.

For information, address Harvest House Ltd.
4795 St. Catherine St. W., Montreal,
Quebec H3Z 2B9

Printed and bound in Canada.

Designed by Robert Reid.
Cover illustration by Gil. de Cardaillac.

The Publishers gratefully acknowledge
a translation grant from The Canada Council.

Ah! How the old sagas
run through me.
Herman Melville *Mardi*

to child ô

. . . .
. . . .
. . . . .She was looking
out the window. The Old Man was listening
to the radio, wiping his glasses. His hands
shook. One finger always moved haphaz-
ardly settling on his glass. The Old Man
persisted because he did not like to wear
dirty glasses; once he understood that
he would not be able to clean them, he
let his long arms fall, sighed and yawned. He imagined himself a huge cat and felt
the sun's warmth on his skull for the first
time. He pushed the easy-chair a little,
set his legs on the footstool and closed his
eyes. His hand felt through his shirt pocket;
he put his glasses away. "I think I'm going
to take a nap." The woman said nothing,
she never said anything so long as she
wasn't angry with him. She rattled her
dentures, shrugged her large shoulders,
dipped her fingers into the soapy water and
began again to wash the dishes. There was
a song on the radio which she liked. It
reminded her of a forest of great black

trees with bears and elephants. She did not know why there were always elephants with big ears in the songs she heard. It was maybe because of a picture in a book, or a film, or a story that the Old Man had told her. She was so distracted now; she lost her train of thought so easily, as if she were the victim of several disconnected ideas at once, letting herself be invaded by all kinds of words that exploded in her and scattered everywhere. The Old Man slept in his easy-chair. (Dribble was running down his chin. His foot had a tic: every ten seconds his skinny leg shook violently under his trousers.) "It hurts," thought the woman. "It hurts in my stomach. Maybe that's what death is." She wiped her hands and put them on her stomach. She thought of a religious ceremony and saw a man in black touching her stomach. She saw a priest kneeling before her. Running his fingers over her, he was saying: "That's death in your stomach, Milienne honey. You needen't get excited. Death is long sometimes, it wants to live before ending." She put her hands back in the water. Thinking about death didn't frighten her. No elephant's ears came to mind like when she listened to songs on the radio. There was a kind of peace, as if death were already present in the gestures she made: in the water that squirted from the milk bottle

when she stuffed the old dishrag through
its neck, and in the sun that came through
the window, making a column of light
where the golden specks of dust were
swarming. Suddenly her stomach hurt her
very much. Tears came to her eyes. She
clenched her teeth. "He'll never know that
I'm letting death settle in my stomach
now," she said to herself, sniffling. She
turned her head and looked at him. The
Old Man's skull was a ball of white hairs
that grew in disarray. "Is his stomach
dying on him too?" she asked herself.
She felt ashamed of thinking that and turned her head away. She hadn't any more
dishes to wash, but she could not take her
hands out of the water; she played with
the soap bubbles, and they burst, making
small noises, "cicada noises," she thought
mockingly. A soothing warmth rose up her
arms, followed the line of her neck, mounted her jaw, filled her nose and took hold
of her head, making her recall some sweet
faraway emotion. "It's true, I *am* old,"
she murmured. She lifted one hand out of
the water — the gold band was shining
because of the soap — she found that her
tapered unwrinkled fingers were beautiful
still. She had always thought that if her
fingers did not come apart like the rest of
her body, she would not die. "If it were
not for this cursed stomach." She pulled

the plug from the bottom of the sink and the greasy grey water slipped away. There was a whirlpool in the middle of the water, a cabbage leaf wheeling round on the surface. Now Milienne looked on without thinking of anything, her mind free and empty as when, in former times, she couldn't sleep beside the Old Man who snored and rattled his teeth. The sink pipe belched and she thought that that would wake up the Old Man, but he was sleeping soundly, his mouth wide open. He had only one tooth left and he always kept his tongue on it as if he wanted to protect it. Milienne did not know what displeased her suddenly about the Old Man, maybe his stomach, she thought. His stomach was flat and hard, with four creases of muscle and long white curly hairs. She regretted that she had married again. She knew that the Old Man regretted it also. But they didn't say it to each other. They kept it within themselves, perhaps, so that they wouldn't suffer too much, and to give themselves the illusion that there had been something beautiful in this process that had one day brought them together. (She was digging in her garden when the Old Man had come up behind her and placed a warm hand on her hip. She remembered that well because it was the first time that he touched her, that he placed his hand on her, a huge old hand she had found sad because of the scars and the wart on the thumb. The Old Man had said: "Wouldn't you like it Milienne, if you could sleep beside me all the nights that the two of us still have to live?" She had not understood right away. She thought it was the sun heating her back and the wind in the leaves that had carried the Old Man's voice from far behind those trees that were completely red. Then she straightened herself up. The wind flattened her skirt against her thighs and he smiled at her, looking at the men's boots she always wore when working behind the house. Then they had gone inside. The kitchen smelled of cabbage. She made coffee for him, which he liked strong and without sugar, and they listened to the radio, motionless, side by side. The Old Man lapped up his coffee like a cat. More-over, it astonished her that he always spoke about cats which she identified him with when he drew out his tongue and made tlap! tlap!' sounds with it as it touched the hot coffee. And his bushy eyebrows that rose straight up to the middle of his forehead, and his mustache like horns on either side of his mouth. She had said to herself: "Well, shouldn't I call him Minet," but she didn't follow up this thought. She never did what she believed she was going to do. Either she forgot or she put it off till later or, when she thought of it again, she found that it didn't make much sense.) The sun hurt her eyes now. Milienne wandered away from the window, wiped the arborite around the sink, opened one hand and threw in the dirt that the rag had accumulated. Then she placed her foot on the pedal of the garbage pail and it opened wide as a cat's mouth. An all-pervading odor of rancidness and rot pinched her nose. (Outside, there were the familiar raucous voices of children cutting across the field on their way to school. They would have red apples in their hands and a school-bag on their shoulder and small shoes that were either shiny or dirty, and ruffled hair and butterfly bows they took off as soon as they'd left the house and kept in their pockets till they reached the school where the bell was already ringing like a big whimsical bumblebee. They were reassuring, these daily, un-changing things: there was peace in them, and goodness too, Milienne thought. "If the bell wished to, it would stop ringing, or it would cry death. Why shouldn't a bell cry when we hit it since there are weeds that cry when you pull them up?" She had read that a good long time ago, but her memory was good for details like that. That one came to her straight from childhood; for a moment, a gust of heat rose up to her face and made two pink blots on her cheeks. She closed her eyes, for black spots had begun to dance in front of her and her heart made something like a leap in her chest.) She was so small suddenly, and so round, and all white in her long dress. She was walking in the path facing the house and she was singing because it was nice out, because there was sunshine everywhere and the grass smelled good and the calves were playing in the alfalfa fields, their tails straight out as if they were being followed by a swarm of wasps. Why couldn't this peace have lasted forever? There was a muffled sound in Milienne's stomach. She thought that something had just torn inside her. Blood was gushing from a wound. She saw a kind of red broth that was cooling somewhere in her stomach, and she would have liked to let it rise within her and vomit it in the sink. (What kind of stain did death make as it flowed softly down the rusty pipe?) She took hold of the cupboard and closed her eyes, terrified suddenly. Needles pierced the skin of her stomach, blocked up her veins and moved up to the heart. (Spears of savages breaking the air's tranquility and driving themselves in-between naked shoulder blades.) "My God, my God," she thought, "could it be that I'm dying this soon?" She did not want to scream to free herself from her anguish, for she was afraid of waking the Old Man. He needn't know, not now or ever. She would never speak to him about her stomach and what was happening there and what she thought about it. She thought of much blood, all the images of blood in her life came loose in her head with a violence and a fury that emptied her of all her strength. She fell into a sticky world and was carried off in a whirlwind of swollen, decomposing stomachs. All kinds of sounds came to her ears, twisting inside her body. Milienne opened her mouth. (A fresh-water fish thrown into the brine of a big lard barrel.) Her hands left the edge of the cupboard. Slowly she felt herself sliding to the floor, seized by a dark force that was breaking her eardrums and that would make the blood gush from her mouth. Then she started to cry silently with the sleeve of her old dress covering her face, ashamed and incapable of getting up. Everything had begun to turn: she herself was turning like a red top. Everything was colors, sad songs, and agony. And her stomach was the black flower of a used-up woman, "My God," she said, "I'd *much* rather die." She crawled along the floor up to the table, gripped the leg of a chair and tried to sit down. But the chair toppled to the floor. (Was it possible for a chair to fall that hard?) And Milienne understood that the order of the world had just changed brutally; that the kitchen and her house and the street and the big trees full of fruit, and the church whose steeple could be seen from the window, Milienne understood that something obscure had just smashed all that, and that soon there would be only despair in its place, a terrifying stomach-ache that would stop and prevent any new act of creation. The world had come out of her stomach in disgusting smells. It had left her alone and suffering on a floor soiled with bread-crumbs. At the other end of the kitchen, the Old Man's cat was lapping its milk out of a bowl. (That pink tongue drawing out and back into its mouth.) Milienne grimaced. She hated cats. She hated the Old Man. She hated her stomach that was like a sponge soaked with pain. "But I've got to get up." She attempted to use the table for support, but her hands had no strength. All her life was being used up in her noisy breathing. She opened her mouth, still she couldn't cry. Then she bit her fingers and broke down into sobs, wasted and used up. She was no longer Milienne, but something frightful, pie-dough rolled out clumsily on newspaper with one red eye hugely swollen and burning; or a long worm, a hideous intestine filled with dirt. She gasped. She was drowning in a whirlpool and the Old Man, who had wakened, was watching her leave. The whirling of the black spots in her eyes accelerated. Before losing consciousness, she had only the time to cry: "What's that you said, Milien?" . . . .

. . . .
. . . . Still, the Old Man had not opened his mouth. He saw very well that Milienne was rolling on the floor, but he was incapable of going to her, to speak to her and help her. His dreams were still all warm inside him and he did not want to make them rise up like a flock of wild ducks. (The young woman's two naked legs remained open still, obscenely showing the pink crack of flesh and the fleece of black hair. And he himself had placed his hand there to hear the young woman laugh and to take from her the coins that made a silver column straight up her vagina. The young woman laughed heartily. Her very white teeth were shining, her stomach was soft and her navel was a shadowy hole at the heart of it; and Chien Chien Pichlotte sat there in the middle of the navel, eating melted butter.) The Old Man wiped his mustache with the back of his hand. There was the taste of soup in his mouth. "Too greasy," he thought. "She makes her soup too greasy." The figure on the floor had not

moved. It made a black stain on the kitchen tiles. The Old Man remained seated. Something stronger than himself, hate maybe, prevented him from going to his wife to comfort her in her suffering. He took his glasses from his pocket, put them on his nose and patiently looked for his cane which she must have placed in the clothes closet while he was sleeping. The big yellow cat was now rubbing itself against his legs. It was purring. The Old Man pushed it away with the tip of this boot. The cat drew away and began licking its fur. In the sun its eyes were like golden circles that almost completely enveloped its face. The Old Man got up, the bones in his legs cracking; he felt like crying because he could not master the kind of anger that had engulfed him. He thought of his cane and imagined himself in the act of beating the body spread out unconscious before the cupboard. That scared him. This violence that was rising within him scared him because, beneath it, there was surely hiding some terrible design. "Milienne, Milienne," he said to himself. "But what's wrong with you, good God. What's happening to you, eh?" He crouched over her and placed his hand on Milienne's shoulder. He was no longer capable of touching her. She was so thin now. Her bones were so hard under the dress and there was so much

cold under those old slack muscles. "Milienne, Milienne!" he said, kneeling before
the motionless figure. And the Old Man saw
the trickles of blood that had coagulated
on her lips. That made his heart beat,
made him take hold of the chair with his
two hands for support. "Milienne is dead.
What am I going to do with her now?"
(He'd begun by hitting her lightly on the
shoulder up to the moment when something
broke inside him, some thread of goodness,
and all his scorn and temper came out
suddenly in the blows that he was deliver-
ing with the flat of his hand. The Old Man
was panting, incapable of stopping himself,
and his fists were the pistons of some demented machine that would stop only when
it broke down. The black stallion was
prancing, kicking because of the bit sawing
into the pink flesh, and neighing because
the Old Man was whipping its haunches
with the reins: "I'll get you. Oh, this will
teach you! I'll get you all right." And the
horse kicked, pranced, snorted, stubborn
and indomitable, its eyes full of malice. The
Old Man flew into a rage and mutilated
the beast, jabbing the pitchfork hard into
its kidneys. It was the satisfaction he got
from drawing blood that scared him. The
stallion's penis was like the movement of
blood itself, a red-hot fury at the sight of
which his rage collapsed. There was no

longer anything but tenderness between the stallion's legs, its big phallus was a force against which the pitchfork was both powerless and ridiculous.) "Milienne, Milienne," the Old Man repeated. "Wake up." And, weary suddenly, he added: "You'd be a lot better off sleeping in your bed, Milienne, honey." A great weariness was burrowing into his shoulders. He had never felt so tired and so totally indifferent to what was going on between Milienne and himself, as if everything which was false in them and between them, had wholly filled the air, disfiguring their motionlessness and their silence, spreading terror in every direction. They had always fled each other and were going to take each other's lives now as if by some mysterious decree. "I'm sorry," he thought. "I shouldn't have hit you, Milienne." He rose, walked to the clothes closet, took out the cane that he had carved from a tree branch and sculpted and painted black. He slipped on his vest and went out after turning off the radio. (His last vision was of Milienne lying in a small pool of blood, her eyes shut, her legs folded under her: Milienne in a humble posture which was itself an act of accusation, despairing in its motionlessness.) (He thought of the large jutting veins and the straight black hairs on her twisted legs; he looked at

Milienne's shoes, her dark stockings. Whenever he saw Milienne's legs, the Old Man always thought of stakes, and he imagined them sinking into the ground and disappearing under the weeds. "How come I accepted that?" he said to himself, pushing at the door's latch.) Outside, everything told him that Milienne wasn't going to die, for there was too much sunlight and too many birds in the red trees, too much dust in the streets and too much water in the Boisbouscache River. The Old Man forgot that he must go fetch the doctor. He had thought that when he returned to the house, Milienne would be awake and, as always, she would be dusting the cupboards. "You don't kill that kind of person just like that." He took the shortcut that led to the church. He kept his eyes on the path because his legs were no longer very supple and he almost lost his footing at every uneven spot. (Maybe he was like Chien Chien Pichlotte, and his head turned round while a collie's long brown coat pushed up against his rear.) He mumbled. He wanted to think of nothing; he wanted to free his mind from everything that was suddenly confusing and dirty. But he couldn't: at one point, it was a faucet that wouldn't shut right and its dripping gave him nightmares in his sleep; there was the barn that caught fire, scorched pigs' hair; children's screams, fuel cans exploding, making his ears ring; there was the sky tearing itself open, streaked with great blue thunderbolts, and Milien thought of a radio, an old stately set that belonged to the Fortins; he thought of the lightning bolt exploding in the wire grating, and of his friend tragically electrocuted. (He died after much suffering; he died horribly, and insane.) They had tied him to his bed and gagged him, not to hear the screams and curses. The Old Man had seen him die. They had just made him drink and suddenly he opened his mouth and his white tongue stretched out and his jaws snapped shut. The small tongue tip fell onto his chin; his protruding eyes became all red, and this was how he went, there in the room with the blinds pulled down, his big wild dog sleeping in the chair. (Leather straps over the stomach. The death of a rabid beast. The beautiful muscles frozen in a gesture that would never be repeated.) The Old Man trembled. He had promised himself never to dredge up those horrifying memories again; there were too many of them, they would take up all his time and end by devouring him. They flew above him and in him like black flies. He had crossed the path now and was walking in the asphalt schoolyard. The volleyball nets were stretched between the posts and he amused himself by following the white lines drawn on the asphalt. Once even, he almost fell over after making a leap so as not to miss a line; he picked up his cane, lifted his hat which had slipped down over his eyes, and continued his walk while avoiding the white lines. He didn't see the school yet. Some days his eyes kept him in a kind of fog of changing colors; at twenty feet he could no longer distinguish things which assumed bizarre forms, exactly like when Milienne took photos with the old Kodak. That happened two or three times a year: she infallibly photographed the house, the chain of poplars surrounding the lot, the cats she detested, the field, the church steeple pointing upward at the end, and Milien standing on the sidewalk in shirt sleeves, his big suspenders like a yoke encasing his shoulders. But Milienne did not know how to take photographs, and all her pictures were out of focus: blobs of colors, shadows overlapping, twisted trees like smoke escaping from the bowels of the earth. The Old Man stopped. He took out his checkered handkerchief, wiped his eyes, closed them for a moment to escape the sun. He must have been near the school because he heard children's voices and music. He lifted his head: a great shady spot lay before him, maybe a hundred feet away. He directed himself toward this black wall. He could see fairly well now. He held the cane in his hand and from time to time he pushed his hat up with its nob. The hat had been sliding down over his head ever since he'd removed from the lining the small piece of newspaper he'd put there. It hadn't been long since he left the house. But for him it had been hours. Since his eyesight had been fading, he hadn't the same perception of time which either stretched or shrank, as if, along with the distortion of what he saw, there needed to be added within himself the distortion of what he feared. Sometimes even his body deceived him. Its movements were exaggerated and he had the impression of having monstrous arms and hands in which Milienne was wholly swallowed up when, overwhelmed by some vague feeling of tenderness, he would put his arms around her to embrace her. Or else his head became large, so large that his body was like a wart stuck to its skin. That also scared him. For years he had moved so little by himself that these transformations forewarned him of a menace that was beginning to inhabit him and nourish itself on his old flesh. (He would not be able to hold out for long, for a few hours perhaps, up to the moment when he would crack up for having braved the sun for too long.

He would go blind, crushed under great hardship; he would become a frightened beast, flattened out in the brush, grovelling in the pool of piss behind the barn with a Winchester bullet in one lung.) He dismissed this thought, bit his lips, struck his leg once with the cane. "Go on, you old work-horse," he said to himself. Then he walked up the steps to the church, pushed the heavy door, took off his hat and crossed himself while his eyes adjusted themselves to the subdued light. Pot in hand the verger was pouring holy water into the basins. The Old Man whispered to him: "Do you think the flowers will be to your liking this year?" The verger shrugged his shoulders and disappeared behind the confessional (a big jack-in-the-box where impurities fought silent wars in the absence of the priest who was counting wine bottles under the sacristy steps). The Old Man walked up the central aisle where the red carpet was like a dried tongue. The verger reappeared. This time he held a bag in his hand. The ring of keys was beating against his thigh. The Old Man had raised his eyes and was looking at the cupola, the prisms of colors made by the stained-glass windows representing the evangelists. Angel heads sculpted in fake marble columns were smiling in the gilding. Peace flowed from their eyes and ran down the walls to adorn the solitude of the Old Man on his knees. The verger stopped before the poor boxes and unbolted them. The money jingled in the bag and the Old Man felt reassured. At least *that* had not changed. He thought of large coins, the kind he gave to his grandsons when they entered the house and shook hands after the long trip. He was in the first pew and he kept his small eyes fixed on the flame burning in the sanctuary lamp. When his knees hurt, he sat down. "I ought to pray now." He took his rosary from the leather case, his lips started moving. He was going to stay there in the darkness for as long as it would take to merit three hundred days of indulgence. The Old Man never prayed for himself; he had too many children who were dead and in need of indulgences. Today, for Mathilde, he would stay a long while in the church. She'd been dead six months now and her coffin, after having been stored in the vault behind the church, had been put in the ground in the family plot where it would rot in the sunless underground in company with the other members of the clan. The Old Man wept, his indulgence notebook open before him. On each page he had written the name of one of his children, and, under each name, he had inscribed the days of indulgence he had won for them with

his prayers. "I'm behind on Lucienne,"
he thought. Then he sank wholly into the
labyrinth of prayers he contrived while
falling asleep ....
....
.........................After he had
prayed for a long time, he fell asleep on
the bench. He was more and more attracted
to sleep. He had the impression that by
sleeping a lot, he wouldn't really die; that
these imaginary deaths would deliver him
from what would happen once he had left
the church. When he awoke he always felt
a little lost; if he had not dreamed, and
if he did not look at his large watch, he
could not say how long he had slept. It
was five minutes, perhaps, or an hour, he
did not know. That astonished him. And it
worried him, for he was not certain he
could find an answer to the questions he
was asking himself. Moreover he had believed from the beginning that it was only
through his imagination that he would
destroy the cancer which was taking possession of his mind and making him like
a stranger to himself. He had never
thought that he would become the prey of
dreams in his old age, he who had always
kept away from dreams because reality
was much more attractive. Daily life
swarmed with ready-made dreams. You had
only to cast aside your reserve and to look

a bit farther than the tip of your nose to become aware that dreams inhabited the entire landscape and that, beyond Saint-Jean-de-Dieu, nothing of this world's truth existed. Everything was taken up by new life forms that gleamed like big cars, or were as dirty as factory chimneys, or painful as legs crushed in the flesh-eating reaping machines. That's why Saint-Jean-de-Dieu had to be surrounded with its fence of stately cedars; that's why you had to pray a lot in your old age to keep the devils away. But that wasn't easy, for the nightmare was sly and came in a thousand disguises that too often made him pass sleepless nights now, terrified by the flow of delusive images rising within him to his destruction. Resistance to them was perhaps an even greater danger, and in the end he would lose himself, hopelessly dispossessed of the beautiful things that had filled his life. At night, someone within him whom he did not recognize, dreamt of an ugly country swollen with an evil life that was going to take hold of everything in the world he knew and loved, and waste it and leave only large vicious cats in its place. (The angels had left the marble columns and were flying through the church, their transparent wings beating in the emptiness. Oh, how beautiful the hymns were, coming from those round mouths.)

When the Old Man awoke he understood that a curse was awaiting him; he was going to die in a small room, alone and hated by the people in his house. That night in his sleep, he must have made sharp movements, because his watch had fallen from the little table onto the floor and its hands had stopped. The Old Man became fearful and was unable to fall asleep again. Anguish had compressed his stomach and he could barely breathe. He thought that he was sinking into the center of his bed, or that the walls of his room had started moving as in a dream, or that his whole body was a wash-board, deforming his face, twisting his nose, and enlarging his ears. To escape the curse, he had dressed himself in the dark, taken his hat and cane and walked out. There was fog outside and the wind that was blowing calmed him a little. Dry leaves crackled under his feet. He walked like that for a time and crossed the entire village, reaching the road that led to Route 8. Then, in his mind he made the rest of the journey; he walked for about twenty minutes more, descended the hill to Elie and gazed at the covered bridge for a long time. At Epinette's slope, a rustling black ball caught his attention; cows were grazing in the field; a horse was sleeping with its head against a railing; an albino bull was mounting a female and, before a thicket of trees, a flock of sheep with long yokes tied to their necks were slowly chewing the grass. It was dark still, and there was fog, but the Old Man could see everything. He had made this trip so often that he no longer really had to look. All the pieces of the puzzle were in his head. When he reached the end of Route 8, the Old Man took the side road. He was especially careful for most of the small bridges here were broken and the road was full of holes. He began to sing; he liked to hear his voice. It seemed to him that his voice was not quite the same in the dark. He quickened his step so as to arrive at Rang Rallonge before the break of day. He no longer wanted to see his land except in darkness. Otherwise he would not recognize it, as if he'd never lived there, as if, taking the wrong road, he had lost his way. Of course, he knew very well that if he kept walking in a straight line he would reach Saint-Médard, and if he turned to the left, he would go toward Saint-François or Saint-Eloi. Wasn't this where he had lived his whole life. Oh, there were no longer the great aspens before the house and the barn had been re-covered, but the rest was more or less unchanged... yet it was not at all like before. Maybe his eyes were deceiving him or perhaps the world had really changed. Children were running through the fields, and they were his children. It was Mathilde, still small and plump and laughing, a pail in her hand as she came toward him. She was calling to him, out of breath from so much running — no, he did not remember Mathilde's words; he had never payed attention to what children said. Then he walked up to the edge of his land. The tiny stream was still running between the wild hazelnut trees, the polished stones were green, and in the crack of a rock, an old dented cup lay rusting. No one would drink from it anymore and no one would trim the brush that grew like a forest on the land that had been left to itself. The Old Man walked on a bit and stopped to wipe the sweat from his face. His old checkered handkerchief was dirty and he threw it into the stream. The Old Man thought of a bloodstain and everything suddenly changed within him. He no longer heard the birds, nor the drawn-out whistles of the groundhogs, nor the cows bellowing, nor the sound of water passing over stones. Now there was only silence, a kind of fear charged with memories. He thought that it had settled in forever, and that his feet, in sinking into the earth, had become white milky roots, and that these roots burrowed ceaselessly into the clay, exploding underground rock, drinking water and devouring the blind beasts that lived in the secrecy of this enormous belly. And the farther the roots went into this belly, the more they sank into the whiteness, becoming whiter themselves. They would finish by melting into this belly into which they'd intruded. The Old Man saw networks, patterns, knots; all this reminded him of a ball of wool thrown into the kitchen to amuse some black cats. He tried to move his feet but couldn't move them. He was swallowed up into the earth, sucked by the roots and drawn under toward this whiteness where it would feel good to stretch out, and where it would be good to pray for all his children who had died far from him and so long ago that he would never be able to recognize them when they opened the casket's lid in the funeral parlor. All his children were dead now and he himself was clinging to the edge of his land, which was at the end of the known world. (He had begun by removing his shirt because it was hot. He looked at the white hairs on his chest, took his axe from under a pile of leaves and began working in a rage. He had always detested brush and caterpillars that made their nests there, destroying the leaves. When he looked at the colony of caterpillars, thousands of worms well-shaded in their transparent envelopes, he felt himself grow hot with anger. He imagined what these caterpillars had been doing in his wife's belly. She had died because of them, these hideous beasts that had eaten up the whole inside of her body, drying her up and giving her those great mad eyes which remained the only thing he remembered about her death. But now he was very old, his legs got tired so fast and after barely an hour he had to work on his knees, panting with exertion so that his eyes hurt him, filling up as they were with black caterpillars. Then the axe fell from his hands and he began to cry, ashamed of having lost all his strength at a time when he needed it so badly. Sweat was running down his neck and he remained on his knees to punish himself. Then he crawled toward the cabin and threw himself on a bed of leaves. No one would come there to find him, and the pot of *greaves* and the bread on the shelf were mouldy now.) The sound of his rosary falling on the floor woke him. He crossed himself and yawned. Everything was so calm here, so far away from life, from the stream, and the brush, and the caterpillars, and the white roots. Yet the church was also a belly. But it was a black belly in which the imagination turned round, tiring itself and tiring itself so much that one needed the exorcism of prayer to be freed from it. The Old Man muttered yet a few more obscure psalms.

After which he rose, deposited his rosary in the leather case, left the pew, crossed the aisle, pushed the door open and walked around the church. (Spiders were sliding between the stones; toads were leaping through the cut grass to escape the sun.)

. . . .
. . . .
. . . . It smelled of manure in the cemetery. The Old Man walked between the trees, his cane sinking into the soft earth. This was surely a beautiful spring; the grass was completely green already and the leaves, which were as big as your little finger, were rustling in the trees, and there were the new tomato plants that the verger had planted at the other end of the cemetery between two rows of yellow flowers. Far ahead of him in the field, the Old Man saw clouds of dust lifted by the tines of d'Auteuil's chisel plough. Sometimes the wind carried toward him the sharp sound of blades scraping stone. The drone of the great tractor was so regular that finally one no longer heard it. The Old Man picked up a soda pop bottle-cap from the gravel road. He put it in his pocket even though it was rusty and dented. Since he no longer had anything to do and the days stretched themselves out in their monotony, he had the time to be interested in all sorts of things.

Thus he often felt the urge to begin making toys; his father had made them before him, through the long winters of snow. When it stormed and everyone they knew had disappeared in the white cold his father would bring him to the shed where they stored the farm tools. Once there, they had to climb the ladder up to the loft where big quarters of beef and pigs and the carcases of turkeys and chickens lay spread out frozen on a bed of newspapers. His father would say: "Before leaving, we mustn't forget to bring along some pork-tongue and some meat for the roast." And he would clear the table by piling the meat on the floor. Then he would light his pipe, take out his tools, set a block in the vice and begin to sculpt that impossible horse with uneven feet which he would give to one of his sons at Christmas. He would also make a buggy and a harness which he'd color red, and he would go into the barn for a handful of hay, cut it into bits, and place it in front of the horse. While doing all this he would not say a word, absorbed entirely by his sculpture, his unlit pipe between his teeth. ("Me," thought the Old Man, "I was sitting on the edge of the table, leaning my head on the pieces of meat and playing with the pompon on my tuque. Or I would dream. Or I would think about when I would be big.

How many years to wait still? Pa would say to me: "When you can kill a pig, bleed him right, like a man, then I won't need to worry about you no more, Milien." And I could see that, but it was never in the winter, but always in the spring. There was a mountain of logs before the house, a great pile of sawdust and, under the pile, some snow that wouldn't melt. It was the air that had changed. You didn't breathe it the same way. I always felt like running and shouting, my eyes full of tears because of the wind. And the Boisbouscache had flooded over; there was water right up to the wood pile before the house. It was really beautiful, all that water, those heaps of ice, those dead carcasses stranded along the river, those great trees, waterlogged and leafless. Near the dairy there was a cow that had died in giving birth. That morning I'd walked into the stable and seen the cow, her big paws stuck up in the air and the horns caught in the collar and the muzzle bloodied. Under her the dead calf was lying in its sheath. Filled with sadness, I touched it. It was cold already; the calf's head was crushed, and it was *my* cow that had gone. Her big tail full of the piss she would whip into my face. The little teat. That was why I pulled it myself. Pa's hand was too big, and it took him too much time.") The Old Man removed his hat. His hair was all wet. He sweated a lot. He sponged his forehead with his handkerchief and said to himself: "I musn't think about all that anymore; better I should think about Mathilde, about others too, about Milienne." He shivered. (What was it that Milienne had asked him to buy when he went to the general store?) He had forgotten what had happened in the kitchen. His memory was now like a kind of well he no longer had the courage to descend into and repair the cracks of; he had to let the water flow away from now on and not try to imprison it. The water had found its way out all by itself, and perhaps it would even come back into the blackness of his memory as it sometimes happened with his past. Its fragments reminded him that it had indeed happened, that it had once been heavy and fat, but that it was too late to reassemble it all in its entirety. Those big dark holes in his memory didn't scare him, for he knew that the present would be enough so long as his eyes didn't fail him any more. Perhaps if he became totally blind one day, then he would die because everything would be impossible; there would no longer be any refuge for him; time would break down; time would immobilize itself. He was incapable of imagining how things would be then. He had never had very much imagination for that kind of thing. Perhaps he would end up with a knife jabbed deep into his back, the way it often happened in the newspapers. Birds were flying over the great trees, toward the north, to the forests, and peaceful rivers. That had distracted the Old Man. "*What was I thinking about?*" he asked himself. He was now where he was supposed to be, before the headstone where all his tribe's people were buried. There was even his name and date of birth at the bottom of the monument. When he died, Fisette would come with a hammer and chisel and engrave the day, month and year of his death into the stone. That was good. The Old Man knelt down. His knees sank a little into the wet ground. No image came to him. Only this peace, this silence that d'Auteuil's tractor no longer disturbed as it stood still now at the top of the hill. The Old Man thought that maybe that's what death was: no longer to be touched by things, no longer to hear the sounds of the world, to be on one's knees on the wet ground and to remain still and so empty that nothing could penetrate to you, any longer, except by its absence. The death of his children did not touch him today. That was so far off in time that possibly it had never happened. Still, he had sung at Mathilde's burial; as usual he climbed up to

the choir and had taken along his old missal
in its wooden case, and had sat down next
to the organ; he saw the old maid's white
legs and the black object far ahead of him
at the end of the aisle, and the candles,
the priest, and the black thing again. He
began to sing, his knees supported against
the bench. It seemed to him that never
had his voice been so strong and the hymn
so beautiful, and suddenly his throat became clotted; his voice faltered and a
deep sense of guilt rose up within him.
So nothing was certain anymore? So he had
come into a world where everything would
remain forever undetermined? It was
perhaps because he did not ponder his
thoughts long enough, that he hadn't the
time to assure his defense and that it hardly
mattered to him now if he hadn't the energy
to remain faithful to what had once been.
He had felt ashamed in the choir but today
he was proud of himself; his voice had
never been so powerful as at that moment
when the church was infused with silence.
After the organ had made the stained-
glass windows rattle beneath their violet
crepe coverings, it was *his* voice he went
on hearing, and he knew that Mathilde
was grateful to him for this hymn that was
muted and yet sung, for this word of love
that had risen from the bottom of him in
the glorification of her death. (His father

was at the stable door. He was holding a young pig at the end of his arm (there were small tits on its stomach, hardly visible against the skin, and its flesh was whiter near the legs, and its genitals were all swollen, and the pig upside down was squealing, its eyes bloodshot). In his other hand, his father was moving the long knife, its brass-studded white handle gleaming in the sun. He'd said: "Hey, Milien. Come help your father." And Milien, he had walked into the big pool of water; through the hole in his boot you could see his big toe, which was dirty. "Well, go on Milien. Go fetch some straw." He'd taken the pitchfork and gone into the hayloft. He was careful because one of the cats had just had her kittens and they were hidden some-where in the building — and he took as much straw as he possibly could. He knew that outside he would not like what his father was going to do to the pig, and yet his penis would swell up and beat against his blood-stained pants. "Hurry Milien. Hurry up!" (Too much sun and this con-tempt rising within him.) His father had set the pig down in a pile of straw, and had said to him: "Hold him tight by the ears, this is going to take two minutes." Then he saw the blade, the hand, and heard the pig's squeals; the blood squirted out and his father threw the genitals into the pool of water. The dog came to sniff at the pig, then drew out its tongue to lap up a bit of blood, but his father kicked him in the stomach. The dog had gone away, it had seen the bloody genitals in the pool. And finally he disinfected the pig's wound with a rag soaked with iodine. "You see, Milien, it's simple: you cut there and everything comes out." In two days, there'll only be a tiny scar. At the third pig, his father told him: "It's your turn now." He handed him the long knife, and Milien knelt down without saying anything and held the pig's legs fast. It was so easy: one good jab with the knife and, just for a moment, the pig didn't scream. (Red blood on his hands.) His father had taught him that nothing was complicated and if things got that way, you just had to spit in the grass two or three times for everything to come back to its designated place in eternity.) D'Auteuil's tractor was roaring again in the field. D'Auteuil's sons were picking up the stones that the ploughing had pulled up from the ground; the cart was almost full, its tires must be squashed down. And the Old Man thought that the furrows would be too deep and that the oats would grow poorly. All summer you would see the cart's marks; the oats would not be so very high and would yield little. "Me, I would've picked up the stones before ploughing," he said to himself. He was standing, and he was tired; his pants had two great circles at the knees. He leaned on his cane, took out his watch. It was not yet three o'clock. In the spring, everything was slow, time didn't hurry. (The grass smelled especially good.) The Old Man crossed himself, looked at the last epitaph and walked between the crosses. Once he came to the end of the cemetery, he leaned against a tree, took a small box from his pocket, chose a red pastille and placed it on his tongue. A garter snake was sliding through the grass. The Old Man closed his eyes to escape the sun. He was anxious for the d'Auteuil's to come closer to him. That would tire him less; he could drink a bit of their water and speak to them and dip his hands into the sacks of oats, something he had not done for a long time. And maybe then he would become aware that all was not lost and that one day he would again put on his great apron and that kind of pouch he fastened to his stomach, and that he would walk through the field, singing and throwing handfuls of oats around him. The groundhogs no longer whistled in the woods. The Old Man imagined them at the bottom of their holes: big brown balls with small black eyes. Then he leaned against the tree again. (The world was a grain of oats thrown into the warm earth. The transfor-

mations happened under the moss. The whole country rose out of the grass like a stallion's phallus.) The Old Man believed he could stay there for as long as the D'Auteuil's were out of hearing . . . .
. . . .
. . . . And it had to happen while he was waiting. It was like a hemorrhage in his head. He lost his balance and everything seesawed before him, the green of the trees making a huge stain on his retina. The Old Man struck his head against the bark of the tree; his hat rolled through the grass. (A battered black thing.) He began to pant, his mouth very dry and his cheeks burning. The original pain had risen from his stomach, discreet at first, like a pinch, then it became like a whirlpool in a river. Something new had just deposited itself there, a stone that swelled up in his stomach, making widening circles that would finally take over his whole body. Tears came to his eyes. (And the singing of frightened groundhogs.) "Well, well, am I going to die?" asked the Old Man. The murmuring quieted him a little. He crawled through the grass, looking for his cane and completely crushed his hat by putting his hand on it. A volley of curses escaped him as he spat in the grass. His head was hurting him. That was where the stone was, not in his stomach. He exhaled

42

a deep sigh. He had always been afraid of dying by way of his stomach for he knew that stomachs took a long time to go. It was faster when the head was affected. That would last two or three days maybe, and then he'd lose consciousness. He would only think of his cat, big green eyes staring at the sun. Before breaking, his head would fill up with light, and in a flash, he would fall into the white world at the center of the earth. He would not think about Milienne. Stretched out beside him in bed, she would be panting, her big body frozen still and hurting; she would ask him to put his hand on her hot swollen stomach and he would say: "Do you know that I'm going to leave before you do if you suffer anymore?" And also, no doubt: "I'm already dead; they've chopped down the trees in front of the house and everything we've known is in pieces, it's ruined forever. Sleep. Take all the time you need. Personally, I no longer want to wake up, Milienne, dear." He would close his eyes to lock in as much light as possible. But the sound of the tractor would keep him from dying. He would be incapable of bursting the envelope binding him to his body. The sun had disappeared behind a cloud. The Old Man found his cane again, taking hold of the tree to raise himself. The world was falling back into place; the green stain had left the depths of his eyes and recomposed itself into the poplars at the end of the fields. Far off, the tractor made widening circles around a heap of stones, as if it were in the middle of a pool of water, like a stone thrown from the shore, disturbing the harmony of the Boisbouscache. The Old Man understood that what had happened inside his head, had poured out over everything. The tractor was an immense caterpillar weaving its cocoon in the middle of the field. D'Auteuil's sons would be caught in the gigantic net and the tractor would topple them over and break their bones. The Old Man shivered and bit his tongue. He wanted no part of this anguish that was settling in him, this change that was taking from him the world he knew. (If the groundhogs had not whistled.) "I've got to leave," thought the Old Man. Weren't things going better now? His heart had calmed down; his blood ran inside the many Boisbouscaches of his skin. (The Old Man would catch many fish now that he had his great boots on and could walk out into those pockets the river made along its shores. Sometimes trout jumped out of the water to swallow the long-legged flies whose white bellies must be bleeding inside. The shores had just been lumbered and the cut trees smelled good. Pine needles drying. Explosions of smells. Large

44

bumblebees were circling over him as he stood motionless in water up to his thighs. The large bumblebees never stung you if you knew how to stay calm and didn't move. And the red ball at the end of his fishing rod was an obscene aquatic fruit, a terrifying mixture between a dead eye and a bull's testicle baked in the sun. Now the trout's belly, the small broken eyes, the tail lashing, the sticky hand.) The Old Man had taken out his watch. "Why won't you say three o'clock?" he thought. "I must have broken you when I hit the tree." He put it up to his ear. The ticking had not stopped; the small hand was still running in the tiny circle at the bottom of the watch. The Old Man let himself fall in the grass. His watch rolled onto his foot. All the years that he had cultivated the land. he had never feared anything except drought. Stinking smut got into the wheat, making black growths over the stalks that ended up by breaking. Since he had aged, all that terrified him; all diseases could turn against him and finish him off. Afraid, he tried to think of something else. The world was vast. You had only to think of the world to forget yourself. He had often done that in the past when he ploughed for too long at night and was tired and his hands were covered with blisters from gripping the handles of the old plough; he imagined everything there was once you left the Saint-Jean-de-Dieu road and took some other direction. He liked to dream of that because it gave him the feeling of going far out of himself and seeing many great trees and houses different from his own, and barns with pigs in the muddy yards, and fences, bushes, people. The eye could be immense if you knew how to use it. But his eye was dying. So many things had died in his head since he had grown old. The world was growing smaller and closing in on him; in a little while he would be completely surrounded, incapable of thinking of anything that was not near to him; his words would no longer stretch out in time, they would remain within the space of his body. (He would be something like food in a can.) His big cat was going to give birth soon. He knew how that would come about. All afternoon she would have spasms in the clothes closet where he would make a kind of nest for her out of old blankets; her eyes would be larger than usual, and still more yellow. He would pull a chair up to the closet and rock slowly while reading the newspaper. From time to time he'd remove his glasses, look at the cat and talk to her. She would understand him and answer with short meows while the spasms in her stomach would become more and more intense. It would be hot. There would be hardly any wind. The cat would pant, her tongue hanging out of her mouth. Yet she would not touch the bowl of water he had brought into the closet. The Old Man would say: "You're a good cat and I bet you'll have at least six kittens." He played with the pop bottle cap remembering a childhood game. He placed it on his thumbnail and tossed it. Tired of this game, he put the cap back into his pocket. He looked at d'Auteuil's tractor which was slowly getting closer with each great circle it completed. In ten minutes, perhaps, he would dip his hands at last into the bags of oats. He closed his eyes and began to think of his cat again. This would be her fourth litter if she really gave birth. At her first, it had been difficult because she didn't understand, she was terrified of what was happening in her insides and between her legs. Her body was stretched out like a bow; she looked at the transparent envelopes and the black balls that were moving in the placenta, and she meowed, terrified of the blood staining the covers. He had to help her to cut the umbilical cords and clean the kittens, and then he gently placed the tiny mouths on the pink tits buried in fur. (There now, it is almost dark when he opens his eyes. Black pockets fill the sky and violet bolts streak the bottom of the horizon, making enormous cracks above the aspens whose leaves have turned over. (Ancient images, but still new in his eyes.) Whirlwinds of dust rise up in the field where the d'Auteuils are gathering stones. The tractor disappears from the Old Man's sight while he places his two hands over his brows. Then rain begins to fall. The Old Man picks up his hat, restores its shape with two punches and pulls it down over his head. Now the rain — definitely too cold. The d'Auteuils are running in the field; they'll go shelter themselves under the fir trees that grow sturdy along the edge of the land. The Old Man removes his glasses and has trouble finding his cane in the weeds. And then it all happened at once: thunder, leaves slapping faces, wet smells overturning the world's harmony, twisting the countryside that now begins to resemble the pictures taken with Milienne's old Kodak. The Old Man tried to run, but he immediately felt a cramp in his chest and had to resume walking. The water made muddy ditches in the entryway to the cemetery. Holes would fill up with ooze; corpses would float in their copper-colored coffins, worms would drown in the holes they'd tunnelled. The cemetery's iron gate was clanging. (Those hinges!) All over Saint-Jean-de-Dieu they have taken out flasks of holy water and lit lamps before statues of the Virgin Mary and recited prayers. The Old Man opened the cellar door behind the church. He was blinded. He took out his handkerchief to wipe his face. His heart was pounding too hard against his temples. He was angry with himself because he was unable to run. (But why had she put the cat out? He saw Milienne walking down into the cellar. She was going to take the bucket out of the washtub, fill it with cold water, look for the cover on the table, and then, panting because of the cramps in her stomach, she would climb the staircase. Upstairs she would turn off the light and set the bucket down. Leaning against the door-frame, she would think: "I just hope that Milien doesn't come home before I've finished what's now well under way." She would pick up the bucket again and walk into the Old Man's room. The kittens were sleeping in the clothes-closet, rolled up in a ball on an old checkered shirt. Small hairy things, slippers come to life in the dark. She removed the cover from the bucket, dropped it. The noise woke the kittens. Milienne looked at them. "You're finished," she thought. They could not see yet, but they started meowing, their small sightless heads turning in every direction. Milienne took the four kittens into her big hands and threw them in the water. Then she set the cover back on the bucket. It would take a minute and then

they'd all be dead. With the checkered
shirt she wiped up the pool of water that
had spilled when she threw the kittens in
the bucket. Then she took the bucket
and was going to empty it in the small
ravine behind the house, at the end of the
plot.) The Old Man walked out of the cellar
and started down Main Street. . . . .
. . . .
. . . .
. . . .
. . . . .He did not have to push open the door
of the general store because someone
("Big Gin Jalbert," he thought) was coming
out just as he was walking in. A big whisk-
ered man waved to him from the counter.
He saw the green eyeshade in the middle
of his forehead like a fish scale, and he
heard him say: "Hey, Old Man, do you
want to catch your death?" He did not
answer. There was too much cold all
through his body. Outside, the water puddles in the streets must be covered with
a thin layer of white ice. (The hoofs of
his beautiful brown stallion, the sound of
iron shoes on the asphalt, the ice breaking
— like a window shattered by a stone —
when the stallion ran over it; its ears
stood straight up on its head, and the bit
had made two bleeding cuts on either
side of the lips.) The Old Man rubbed his
hands together. The warmth would begin

there and flow through his entire body, and it would make a pocket of life in his stomach that would protect him from any disruption. Each time a customer walked into the store, a bell rang above the door. The Old Man took three steps and the smoke from a cigar made him sneeze. With his handkerchief he wiped the snot that had fallen into the hollow of his hand. "Listen. Couldn't I have a little something to warm me up." The big man lifted his eye-shade. Behind him the religious calendar had come unstuck at the bottom and was all rolled up into a kind of yellow telescope on the wall. "Go on in back. Emma'll take care of you." The Old Man removed his hat and his sweater, placing them on his arm. He walked up to the end of the store, opened the door on his left that led into a kitchen shining with chrome. No lamp was burning before the blue Virgin Mary on the shelf nailed to the wall. Emma wasn't there either; only the litte dog came toward him, set its paws on his leg and shook its tail, its wide brown eyes shining with contentment. The Old Man bent over and patted the dog. "Ah, it's you." Emma came down the stairs with a basket of clothes in her arms. She was a beautiful girl, and for a long time he looked at Emma's buttocks rounded in the pants that bulged between the legs.

Emma set the clothes down on the table near the electric iron that looked like an over-white misshapen hoof. The dog was playing with the cord, yapping and kicking its legs. When it got the cord into its mouth, Emma stretched out her foot and kicked it. The dog howled and started running, knocked its head on a table and then, turning like a top, it hid under the table piled with dishes. Emma's breasts must be beautiful under her blouse. Like pears ripening on her chest. (Emma stretching out on the kitchen tiles. Her blouse opening over her pears and someone bending over her as she closed her eyes, dreaming of what was going to happen. A mouth opening, teeth biting into one of the pears, then slurping sounds. And Emma laughing — and when the man stood up, there remained only the cores of pears on the young woman's chest.) "I'll have a gin," he said. "I got caught in the storm." (The radio drowned out all other sound. It was forever howling the same songs, the same complaints that penetrated your ears and stuck to you like tendrils or burrs. On the face of it, it doesn't seem like much but it could wound you, tatter your feelings, make your mind extremely vulnerable.) Emma gave him á smile and walked to the cupboard. When she pulled at the knob, the shuttle fell from where it was hooked onto a nail. Not long ago they had had the house repainted and drops of paint had leaked into the hinges. (Those beautiful gold-colored pine walls would be grey from now on.) There was the gurgling of gin in the flask's neck, then the tap's belch. "And here's your sweet child," Emma said, handing the Old Man his glass of gin. The first swallow burnt his throat, made a column of warmth right down to his stomach where it got lost somewhere under the navel. (What was this song that had burrowed into him to end in a corrupt desire?) "It's good," said the Old Man. "Thanks, Emma." She had put a white shirt out on the table and was passing the iron over the sleeves. (A slack skin, like a man's. And will *you* have to die? thought the Old Man.) Then she took a bit of starch from the box, threw a pinch of it into a glassful of water and stirred the mixture with her finger before wetting the shirt's collar. The flesh on her arms shook a little with each stroke of the iron. The Old Man had finished his glass. "You should go dry yourself in the other room," said Emma. The Old Man got up, his knees cracking. "I was doing damn well right here," he said. Emma said nothing. She kicked the dog again because it had climbed onto the small bench and was chewing on a piece of clothing. The Old Man shut the door and opened another. His bones had never hurt so much.

"Well, hello everybody." The Old Men lifted their heads and looked at him. "Well hello, hello, hello," they said together. "Come, sit down. We're missing players." The room didn't have a window, so you always had to have the light on over the table. There were shadows on the walls behind the two players, and legs of ham hanging from the ceiling, and sacks of flour piled up in a corner, and cauldrons, and portraits of public men on another wall; and, in the middle of the room, an old wood-stove whose red sparks you could see through the cracks in the door and, near the stove, a card table, four chairs and two Miliens bent over their cards and tugging at their pipes. "Well, come sit down with us. We've told you we're missing players." The Old Man walked up to the stove, took a log from the box, opened the small door and threw the piece of wood into the fire. There were sparks and the crackling of flames. (Far off in time, the forest was burning at the edge of his land and he was stretched out in the stream, his face covered with red sores, looking at the trees blaze and break like matches.) He said: "I'm going to dry myself first, then I'll play." He drew a chair up to the stove, stretched out his legs and asked: "Hey, Chien Chien Pichlotte's not here?" The first Milien answered: "Chien Chien's real

54

sick." The Old Man said: "That bad?" He pushed his glasses up, they were always sliding down his nose; he opened his mouth but said nothing, except maybe: "I'm really afraid he won't be able to come play with us no more. This dog stuff has gone completely to his head." The Old Man looked at the fire in the stove. "Today's not a good day," he said. And suddenly he felt like crying and letting the tears flood down his cheeks and hearing the muffled sounds of sobs that would come from the pit of his stomach and fall from his mouth like big crippled toads. He sniffled. The world in his head was going to die at the edge of the land, drowned by that river which would flow out of him with a terrible violence, destroying all vegetation and making rocks and barns explode, along with everything else thrown before it to appease it. Curled up like foetuses in their chairs, the two Miliens triumphed in their treachery and compared cards. The Old Man had started to cry, his big shoulders making odd shapes on the wall from the way they were shaking. "Come on, play with us," one of the Miliens could have said. "We'd sure spend our time crying if we were to think only of all those who no longer come to play with us." Only that made the Old Man rise from his chair. The world of the room hid itself before his tear-filled eyes. This world, what could this world be if not a cemetery with black crosses fastened to its joists? So many similar vigils over so many deaths in so many closed stuffy rooms, hot as pigs' bellies opened in the snow. He had always liked putting his hands into steaming flesh; doing that, he appropriated the pig's vitality. He would never be sick and never die, he would remain forever this white old man running in the snow behind his children and Milienne rolling in her fat. He had bled the pig and Milienne was collecting the thick blood in a saucepan; later she would come to fetch the entrails, empty them, and the black pudding would smell good when he came into the house. The dead pig, pulled to the shed, would be lifted onto heavy shoulders and dumped into a bath of boiling water. That's what living was and loving the stink of burnt hairs that fell from the pig's skin when you hit it with the flat of your hand. "Well, what are we playing?" he said. Too many Miliens began talking about too many card games at the same time — no agreement. "Fifty-two cards for the three of us, is that too many people for your liking?" This phrase, a good thing to say in such circumstances, was spoken by none of the Miliens; rather, banalities were spoken: "Maybe we could postpone it till tomor-

row, eh? I haven't the heart for it today."
If they didn't play, they wouldn't talk to
each other at all. The afternoon would
pass in silence, they would look at the
spirals of smoke rising up from their pipes
to the lightbulb, and they would drink a
bit of coke, perhaps, or gin if Emma
thought of them. They would look at the
yellow pictures on the wall, scratch their
noses, grunt and have competitions. Who
among them was the champion? They
would lift their thighs at the same time,
make identical grimaces and farts would
come out, frightened by the rotten egg
smells in their intestines. One of the
Miliens had once won all the Saint-Jean-
de-Dieu fart competitions and when he
began talking about it, he could go on endlessly, full of crafty talk that explored a
hot world, burrowing into a familiar reality.
(To reassure oneself by speaking with three
holes at the same time: *that* was supreme
art. Truths told with the mouth, the genitals
and the anus, the only truths good to
hear — and to smell.) But time, like the
competitions, passed in the end. "Are we
playing, or aren't we?" asked one of the
Miliens. Rain was no doubt falling outside.
The trees would smell good when he went
out and walked on the wooden sidewalk
with Milienne on his arm. But he was tired
and his legs were stiff. He didn't want to

57

leave. He said: "Good, what if we try Nine into three?" He drew up his chair, set his cane on his thighs. (The yellow cat was roaming in the ravine, looking for her babies. She was meowing, her snoot bloodied from the brambles and her tail full of burrs. Big and dirty after the downpour, the Boisbouscache was flowing somewhere between the trees. The cat would keep looking till she found the bucket whose cover had broken when it hit the rocks. She would lick the kittens and lie down beside them, the milk running from her over-full teats. Then she would take the first kitten in her mouth and deposit it on the doorstep and then come back for another. But while she was at the bottom of the ravine, Milienne would put the kitten on a small shovel and throw it in the black water of the Boisbouscache.) "Do you know that it's your turn to play?" said the first Milien. The Old Man lifted his head and threw an ace on the table. "You won't win a hand," he said. One after another the cards fell. A hard fist shook the table and the jack of hearts turned round three times over the cards; Milien stretched out his arm and greedily drew the cards toward him. It would have been natural if this had made some of the Miliens jealous. But they all had other preoccupations. (And Chien Chien Pichlotte's shadow barking

into ears full of white hairs.) What recollection should one use to preserve the image of the Old Man forgetting that it was not just another afternoon, but an occasion of frightening subtlety — that of death which had begun and ended a long time ago in a world cut off from card games, cut off from the small tame Saint-Jean-de-Dieu with its first boorish inhabitants, cut off from the mellow soil swollen with barley seeds which were the joy of birds, cut off from the copper-colored faces of Miliens yet to come, but who would not be born because time . . . .
. . . .
. .(The rest, we could write ourselves.). . . . . . .
. . . . .One day she had said to him: "Why are you still working all the time, Milien honey?" He did not answer. Words spoken to his wife could not constitute an audible answer. Maybe she had never even understood what he was saying; her simplicity was merely a cowardly disguise. Too many disguises were masking the true face of his beast: taking off one was only playing into the hands of a thousand others moving beneath it. Maybe Milienne was too fat. She sat in the chair he'd made for her, leaning her head against its back and looking at him, her eyes hidden behind pockets of fat that had made her ugly with time. Milienne was a mountain

59

sleeping in the kitchen, her big bare feet on the chair rungs. Her flowered dress had lost its color from being washed, but Milienne refused to wear the new dresses he bought for her. (A tender but misunderstood gesture, the cause of many fights yet to come. It made you laugh and cry because it stood alone in a world too vast and devoid of beauty when you looked at it through a veil of tears.) When he brought her dresses, Milienne did not even try them on; she barely looked at them before she folded them in one of the dresser drawers. Later she would cut them into skirts for her daughters. She herself needed nothing but the chair she fell asleep in as soon as night fell. In the beginning, Milien, after having made the rounds of the buildings, given oats to the stallion (a big devil of a horse you could never unbridle, for then he would become a frightened monster and nothing would stand in his way — a fiery monster that disappeared quickly from one's field of vision, losing itself in the woods, leaving nothing behind but the black imprint of iron shoes on the rocky Coteau des Epinettes), closed the rabbits' cages and the small openings to the chicken coop and walked into the house. He took off his shoes, undressed, filled the basin with cold water and washed himself. That done, he put on clean underpants, approached Mi-

lienne, took from her the rosary she was
holding between her fingers, placed an arm
under her thighs, another behind her back,
and carried her into the bedroom where
he put her down on the straw mattress;
he undressed her and made love to her in
the dark, excited by her big breasts. He had
never kissed her; kisses didn't touch anything in Milienne, nor in himself. They were
senseless, ridiculous and humiliating acts:
entering a mouth other than one's own
could only be the most abject form of
despair. Milienne came quickly; she then
opened her mouth and gasped. The only
gestures she made consisted in taking his
ears and squeezing them in her hands.
When the pain became too strong, he withdrew after pushing her away violently.
(During all the time he made love to Milienne, the big black devil of a stallion had a
particularly obscene mare under him.) He
had a vivid sense of sinking into a greasy
world that would relieve him of his tired-
ness. But Milienne — she was really fat
now — he dropped her one night while
trying to carry her into the bedroom — he
was very weary that night because the cow
had lost her calf — Milienne had hurt
herself. She screamed and shouted something very rude to him, and he was so tired
that he left her there and spent the night
on the doorstep. Then he didn't come to

her for a long time; perhaps Milienne's breasts didn't exist after all. And maybe her fat would melt in the spring. Sometimes he thought what a shock it would be for him if one night, while making love to Milienne again, he were to discover beneath him a woman all made of bone, without those fat legs through which he could no longer disappear. "Rest yourself, Milien dear." That sentence he heard so often would no doubt become all that would be left to him of Milienne. (His father had been so right in telling him that life was a simple, easy thing. You just needed to have time on your side, to know what you could do and what you couldn't do. All the rest didn't concern him in any way. During the day there was a lot of work to do, and at night he dreamed beside Milienne's sleeping form: pigs, and cows without horns, smells of hay in the barn, giblets, piles of stumps, autumn crops, the river, winter repairs on the house foundations, the vegetable cellar where cabbages were yellowing and carrots grew soft.) The carrots must contain a white liquid that drains away before the end of winter. It was like when he withdrew from Milienne, turned onto his stomach and fell asleep his mouth open and dribbling. (Or a game with the dog, or armfuls of wood drying in the small shed behind the house. Before taking an armful of maple logs, he pissed on the floor, overtaken by a great peace — the moon completely round in the cloudless sky, the calves making grey blotches under the trees, fireflies throwing their light through the picket fence. Years would pass, changing nothing in their lives; uniform and slow, time would flow and it would have no hold on them. Cans of cream were let down into the cold water in the wells, the warm milk turned in the centrifuge and the long cats came running. Setting their paws in the buckets, they stretched out their tongues and lapped up the milk to take their fill. In the stable the young pigs were sleeping under the stallion's legs, its rump leaning against the rusty chain.) It was winter, the great February freeze. There was snow as high as the houses' doors and the broken windows he'd blocked up with cardboard. He spent his days in the stable: he combed his cows, taking off the thick pieces of dung stuck to the fur on their backsides, and he cut turnips, prepared rations of grain, put molasses into the bowls of water, prodded the enormous bull in its stall. Its organs were an extremely sensitive sack, a painful sack of life withheld. "One day you'll get killed jabbing him like that, Milien." He shrugged his shoulders, spat in the pool of piss behind the bull. And what if this was life:

breathing the stable smells? When he would be old, he would lose his recollection of everything else; he would no longer remember the buildings, nor the animals he had had, those he'd cared for and those he'd killed in the early December frost, except for maybe the bull's cut head that he would see in the snow under the bridge, there where the pigs' unused entrails were making columns of ringworms. In the spring it would stink and the big white worms would infest the carcases that would end up by completely disappearing under a heap of manure. And while he loaded bales of dirty straw into the wagon, Milienne was on her way out of the house, reassuring him because she was as big as ever with her black hair tied behind her head and her linen apron showing the curve of her breasts under her dress. Then he would spear his pitchfork into the manure and lean on it with his elbow and watch her coming, proud of her — she was like a queen on that road followed by an old rheumy-eyed dog with nothing more now than a nose, the rest of his body having passed to the other side of life. He was going to kill him someday soon (tie him to that stake near the manure heap, and fire a bullet into his head). The children wouldn't want Milien to go drown him in the Boisbousca-che. Also, they'd come to take him from

64

Milien and pull the dog by the legs up to the vegetable garden facing the house, and there they would make him stand up in the snow. The dog would freeze. He would be a mutilated Sphinx standing guard all winter before the door. (With an open mouth, and small clots of coagulated blood hidden under the stiff hairs.) Milienne was coming toward him; in each hand she held a bucket of excrement she would empty into the wagon. He sees Milienne sitting down in her chair, her dress lifted above her knees. The chamber pot disappears completely under the fat. Milienne locks her teeth, staring at the palm branch braided into a cross under the calendar. She had always had a lot of trouble with her bowels. The noisy farts explode in the pot and the strong spurt of piss lasts forever, but the odors that come from all that resemble nothing he'd smelled before. It's warm and sinks into his stomach, exciting him, like when he sees dogs fucking in the snow early in the morning when everything is calm, padded, stuffed under the frozen ground, and astonishingly discreet. To push the door's latch and hear the hinges creak, to walk over the crust of hardened snow: that could overthrow the country and alter night's harmony into a kind of unreality he found moving. On the last step of the staircase, leaning against the bannister with his hands in his warm pockets, he let himself be overtaken by the cold and the light coming from behind a curtain of trees and gently floating over that which lay before his eyes. On the picket fence, birds had their beaks hidden in their feathers, eyes filled with white terror. And sometimes, in the middle of the road, between the tracks left by sleds, there were small heaps of steaming turds. And near the doorstep, the dog had mounted the motionless bitch whose bulging eyes and open mouth, yellow fangs and big round back were something mockingly impure that exasperated Milien and troubled him greatly. Exciting himself at the sight took on a hidden meaning in the cold peaceful morning; all the dark forces of the world inhabited that bitch and, because he was observing, Milien would also be possessed by them and have a powerful erection. The dog's tail was shaking, becoming in Milien's private imagery a sickle of hairs cutting the snowflakes as they were softly falling. All the violence of what remained to be discovered in the world was in the two dogs panting on the doorstep. He walked down the final step and approached the dogs. His kick reached the female's side. (First her cry, and then the sound of his kick making the evil forces tumble out of the beast.) The bitch started running, but the male wouldn't unhitch himself from her and ran on with his sweet possession. In this race of the two animals welded together was an anguish that brought back to Milien an old image: he was lying near Milienne, but they were not in bed under the thick covers; they were walking in the field, one behind the other, savages let loose into the new world to pick berries. His eyes remained glued to Milienne's buttocks. She was balancing a bucket on the end of her arms, and this was making a flow of light, a sparkling wheel. How good it felt to be in the heat, to hear the noisy bumblebees and Milienne's heavy breathing, and to let the dark shadows arrange themselves under the branches of fir trees. The fresh-cut grass smelled good, made you wish you were an animal so you could roll in it. Oh, the leaves in your mouth, the yellow caterpillar crawling along the furrow. And one's member like a lightning-conductor piercing the sky. Milien had stretched out his arm. Unzipping the dress tore the curtain in the temple. The mass of milky white flesh appeared. Nothing greater could oppose itself to the night, no tranquility could be more reassuring and more maternal; this desire could only be answered with the swelling of his life, and it could only grow, shattering the old frontiers of the known world. Maybe there could only be this white thing in the field, and maybe all of creation emanated from it, from the inside of its organs, in its laughter and menstrual blood. Milienne let the bucket fall on the pile of rocks; she had turned toward him, already full of night between her legs. She let herself be taken by the silence, wanting him to see how mute and prodigious she could be. When she begins to tremble and places her hands on Milien's shoulders and then on his ears, he caresses her under the buttocks. She locks her legs like scissors round his loins, and this is how they run through the stones and brambles that will leave cuts on their legs. The darkness is a mouth at the bottom of which they will become motionless among the rocks, the pink trout, the manure, the pots of excrement, the dead dogs, the heads of bulls with glistening horns, the barrels of molasses, the grey cats drinking from buckets of milk, the eyes of dead animals, the tails of pigs disemboweled on ladders leaning against the barn wall, the Boisbous-caches rolling their black waters, the picket fences, the groundhogs, the calves, the crushed grass before the door, and all the imagery of heaven: cloud nets, stars and the moon like a marble in the world's pocket, and blackness everywhere else and blackness beyond the idea, and soon there would be oblivion to what was happening, the simple memory of a hand closing over a naked breast, heavy as a bell. (In the room, sleep in the hollow of the straw mattress.) He and Milienne didn't need to remember because the moment belonged to them, even the repetition of the moment was their possession. Everything was in its beginning and nothing would ever go beyond this beginning which held them apart from the masses and far from the claws of the unknown worlds into which Milien's kin had descended, down into lung diseases and the strangeness of cities with factories — enormous, hard, violent American factories. The manure heap was now in the ploughed field; in the spring he would spread it and the hay would grow well, shoulder-high. When he reaped the hay, many fledglings would be killed, but the mower's iron wheels would bury their cries so that there'd be only peace and sunlight as always. The children would come to play in the hay, bringing along wheelbarrows they'd fill with clover, thus imitating his gestures and even the slowness of his movements. Those nights he would enter the house dog-tired and fall asleep while playing with the cats. He'd have no desire for Milienne, whose large open hands upon her stomach were a reassuring sign of chastity. They would love each other in their silence and remoteness and incomprehension. Only when winter had overtaken the house would they have harsh words for each other and sometimes punches, which would slyly threaten them with the new order that their wrath had imposed. At four o'clock Milienne would finally make the awaited gesture, the memory gesture, a powerful thing against which Milien could do nothing, for there was too much strength in this calm simplicity that annulled all anger and intimacy. Staring at the religious calendar, she would lift her hand and say: "Milien, the children will be waiting for you." These words sufficed, for they were the sum of all that could be said and all that could possibly be heard. And he'd remain silent after that, spit on the red embers in the stove, take his clothes off the great rusty nails in the wall, then go out, harness the stallion to the sled and leave in the snow and stillness in the direction of the small school where his children, noses glued to the frosted window, would watch for him coming. (The snow, so much whiteness, like a skin boring into the underground life. Animals in the earth's cold, the blood's slow rhythm, narrow passageways where they would stay caught, frozen labyrinths in which they'd twist themselves and die painlessly. The snow, so much snow, too much snow falling in the sled and over the world. "Snow," he thought.)

The children would climb in behind him and hide themselves under the furs while the stallion would be shitting patiently with its legs wide apart; that filled Milien's eyes with beauty, the beauty of large brown turds making a steaming pile in the snow. The cats had made tunnels in the hay and were watching for mice. Sometimes a tail moved and you heard the terrified squeal and saw the grey thing caught in the mouth. As long as it was possible to fight for blood, nothing could really be lost and every sacrifice had its meaning. "Hey, Milien, the children will be waiting for you." ....
....
...............The cards fell to the table almost mechanically. The Old Man's hand had begun to hurt from hitting the table too many times. He had not lost even once yet. But losing today would not have meant anything; it would neither humiliate him nor make him angry with his friends. In the room, mixed smells of chewing tobacco and of Milien's bare feet were rising. He had removed his boots and set his legs on a chair whose back, turned toward the stove, was hot when Milien set his hand on it. He himself was sweating; he felt as though a Boisbouscache was flowing under his armpits and going to empty itself of all its water before the afternoon ended.

And then, when night fell over Saint-Jean-de-Dieu, he would break into a thousand pieces and make a tiny heap of dust beside the table where the cards, thrown from his hand, had whirled down in silence. The shadows had barely grown on the wall. Two or three times Emma came and sat astride one of the benches she'd drawn up to the table. She liked to watch them play. She brought them three small glasses of gin and they thanked her with winks and lingering looks on what her body had to offer of utmost beauty. The Old Man had not noticed that Emma's thighs were strong; spread apart on either side of the bench, squeezed into the pants, they were the symbol of some indefinable strength. The skin must be pink and strewn with blue veins whose sinuous movement he could follow with his fingertips. The shadow of her breasts too was present on the wall. "I've got to leave," and: "Milienne's waiting for me." They did not answer him for they knew that he would not leave till they had beaten him once. In any case, two loaded revolvers were at each side of the table and they would kill him as soon as he set his cards down, placed his two fists on the arborite and said, while pushing the chair back with his foot, "Whether you want me to or not, I'm leaving." It must be night outside. The horses were frothing before the store's doorway with big eyes like black marbles rolling on each side of their head. He remembered almost tenderly that at the beginning there were next to no houses in the village. From the hilltop, when you put your hand above your eyes to protect them from the sun's glare, you first saw, far ahead of you through the trees, the fields and the rocks and three roads the length of your finger: they were the limits of the known world, encircling the village. They were the borders that protected the tribe from disasters the wind carried from the north. Some days in summer, unknown odors surrounded the village; they came from the river and were full of the smell of dead seaweed the waves had washed up on the shore; but after having gone so far and crossed marshes, forests, grounds and fly-ridden stables, these odors became distorted, as if rotten. In your nose they were the taste of dandelion wine forgotten in some white iron can. And when you turned and saw before you a village contained entirely within your field of vision, you felt reassured; those few houses with blackened boards, the long grass before the doorstep, the chickens, the dogs, the women kneeling in the vegetable gardens, the old lime-whitened tires containing flowers in the flower-beds, and apple trees full of busy bees, and little girls running in the streets, and dirty boys harnessing themselves up to strange vehicles made of old oil barrels, all that and only that, lived with a richness of life. Along the Boisbouscache, the Indians were breaking up camp, pulling up their tents, burying their burnt-out fires in the sand: they were going to travel into the interior of the land. Fleeing in disorder, they would fire their rifles in the air. (Maybe the bullets would not fall and remain in the sky all summer. Maybe, in mid-autumn, they would kill the ducks going south through the clouds.) Emma had yawned and stretched out her legs on the bench; at ankle level the hairs had been removed, no doubt with tweezers. Small red blotches like drops of blood had formed on her skin. But the flesh was beautiful; a button was missing from her blouse and you could see so much whiteness through the crack, that it was like a hard blow to the head. (Near the end. Milienne's yellow skin looked like a nicotine-stained finger.) In what way could it be understood how, opening his eyes one morning, he happened to notice that his world had been turned upside-down? Still, nothing had changed. The house had hardly moved throughout the night, nor had they begun running between the trees on the far side of the rocks where, flat on its stomach in the long wet grass, the unknown was lying in wait. Nor had the animals changed; the black blotches on his cows were *not* cancers spreading in their fur like an oil slick sinking into the sand. Oh no. Evidently, the stallion was dead; he had found it in the stable, the deformed cold body on the straw, and the pigs it had crushed and smothered under its legs in falling. The Old Man took the scissors out of the cupboard and cut the hairs from the mane and the tail; these dry, shiny black hairs would make precious whips or brushes or even curry-combs. After putting the hairs in a box, he brought the log which he used as a chair when milking his cows, and sat himself down in the manger beside his horse. He caressed its head, the vast space between the eyes. The thick neck was really ugly without the hairs that froze or were covered with hoar-frost in the winter when he went into the woods to fetch the logs he'd chopped down (or to cart manure). No doubt that everything had begun to fall apart in this way, and possibly he had not known how to see the omen in his horse's death. Still, Milienne had risen the same time as he did that morning. Spring was as always: dirty patches of snow in the bogs, and that pool of water behind the house. Milienne had said: "We ought to take out the cauldrons for the soap, — eh?" That was why she got up

when he did and put on her blue dress
with white dots and her glasses also, because her vision was failing while her eyes
slowly disappeared behind pockets of fat.
He watched her walking in the field where
he had just set up the tub; she had thrown
some logs in the fire; bones were boiling
in the lye-water; a curious smell rose from
the cauldron, which he breathed for a long
while. Then, turning his gaze from her, he
lit his pipe. The calves were bellowing in
the stable. He took two buckets of milk,
walked up to the trough and emptied the
milk which was still warm; the calves drank
greedily and their tails shook in all direc-
tions. Only one did not want to taste the
milk. He put his snout into the trough and
immediately took it out. The Old Man
jumped into the enclosure, took hold of the
calf by the two ears and pulled it up to
the trough; then he put its head through his
legs and shoved his wet fingers into its
mouth. The calf fought, but the Old Man
had got a good grip; he put its head into
the milk and the calf sucked at his fingers.
(It's almost day and the sun is a great red
eye above the forests.) But here is Milienne
tying a leather apron round her waist. She
stirs the fire under the tub and a pleasant
warmth pricks her legs, runs up her thighs,
(and she thinks of the religious calendar,
the Christian's virtuous death in bed with

good company around him; under the bed
there is hell and the poor damned burning
in the sacred fire with demons and pitch-
forks and horns and long tails that kindle
the imagination and worry it, because of the
symbol's bestiality. As if being equipped
with such an organ could not only distort
a man, but increase his temptation for
nightmares and brutality, not to mention
those corrupt forms, bodies possessed by
evil, vicious bodies that were too beautiful
and so barred us from Christ). With the
great spoon Milien had carved out of a
piece of wood last winter, she stirs the
mixture of bone, lye, meat and water
boiling in the tub. Sometimes she takes
out the spoon and backs up a step or two:
her legs are so hot that the fire cuts deep
into her organs. (The crackling of wood,
the tub being licked by the fire which was
like a multitude of tongues, the heap of
red embers filled with sparks, the strong
vapors from the broth, all this rising up to
her head along with her blood. Maybe it
was *her* fat melting in the great tub along
with the blood and maybe her bones would
shatter in the alkali. Her big hand was
holding the spoon, bubbles were bursting in
the cauldron.) That morning was beautiful.
Everywhere you set your eyes there were
enormous quantities of life suspended up
high as the clouds; soon they would melt

over the earth, destroying its artificial limits and filling it with countless beings and spirits which would change Milienne so much, and even the children still sleeping in that makeshift dormitory up in the attic where five old beds had been set up. Soon Mathilde would open the small attic window, shove her head through the opening and wave her hand. And Milienne would smile at her child, the little girl she had known since the beginning. That tiny pink ball on her mountainous breast remained her only memory of childhood. "Mathilde." She died because one day she had wanted to grow up too much. To think again of the too-many-men that came to the house for Mathilde and forced her into brutal changes, making her too quickly into a full-grown woman, like the recollection Milienne had of her in her memories. In twenty years, Mathilde would be more than her daughter. She would be something like a reconstruction of herself, and it was through Mathilde that she would become immortal, even if her body rotted in the ground. Mathilde now lived in a city at the other end of the world; she got little news from her, one or two letters a year, but something of her was in herself and it would never be lost. It felt good to dream those dreams, and there were so many resources in the imagination and so many possible lives. She had only to look at the soap slowly shaping itself in the boiling cauldron, and the bubbles along the rim were signals of recognition; with a glance she could take in the smells of spruce-resin and the birch syrup and the waterfall sounds that magnified the springtime and made it flow over their possessions; it had taken her some time to understand that winter, in its immense whiteness, was a period that stretched out without obstacles, and that summer, with its borders made of fences and its screen of trees and the Boisbouscache River burrowing through rock, modified the world in your eye and contracted space; summer populated the world and Milienne used that as the support she needed to fight the disease which would plant itself in her in the long season, some-where in the area of her stomach, and then suddenly begin to grow. An evil life was invading her from the inside with such violence that it threatened to reduce her anguish that, thus far, she had always kept distant by confirming her secret existence, situating herself more and more in an im-mortality and a silence that Milien had learn-ed to respect. She saw him; he was there, near the dairy. He had placed his excre-ment-stained fingers under his nose and was breathing deeply so that the smell of dung could go far down into his lungs; and the

chickens stretched their necks to the damp ground, rummaged through the balls of clay with their yellow beaks, and clucked with the delicate chicks under them. And Milien was happy; so much white flesh in the morning was a sign of eternity, an immutable sweet thing that belonged to him. She put two or three logs in the fire and made great circles in the cauldron with her spoon; the bones had melted down and soon she would be able to cut out bars of soap with the long knife, and they would harden on the table behind the barn where the orphaned sheep were bleating, their heads stuck through the holes in the fence. When she put her hand before her eyes to see Milien better, she felt a great cramp in her stomach. She had emptied too much lye into the tub and the soap would take hold badly, and it would burn the skin. "Milien", she said in the voice of her secret existence . . . .
. . . .
. . . . .One evening the great chair was left empty in the middle of the kitchen. That struck Milien like a whip when he came in after taking care of the animals in the warm stable. The big yellow cat was sleeping on the cushion, rolled up in a hideous ball. The radio station had gone out of wack and the hoarse sound that was coming from it broke his courage; he was suddenly very alone, and lost, and power-

less, at the mercy of the event that had just overtaken him; the world had shrunk and surrounded him, the kitchen was a dusty enclosure where he sweated while waiting for the mad bull to charge him with its deadly horns and its black eyes. The tip of the horn would get him right in the middle of the stomach, and all of space would enter his wound. "Milienne," he said. He took the cat in his hands and threw it on the floor, then he shut off the radio. Milienne had lit a candle in the bedroom and stretched out on the bed where she was now sleeping with her great mouth open and her hands crossed over her stomach. There was so much tranquil energy within her that Milien was freed from his anguish. He stood a long time in the doorway looking at her. Great tenderness rushed through him, for nothing could really change; they were made to last forever and they would age in this calm slowness, and their aging would bring them only more intensely toward childhood and the deepening of this very childhood from which they would draw their continuance. Somewhere beyond the world, their sons and daughters had begun travelling over so many familiar roads that were marked, stretching out like elastic, so that they could only return to the house from where they had all started; there in the heart of this house they would all join together and sing of their accomplishments. There would be many grandsons and granddaughters, even his father would be there; mustached and white he would be playing with the kids on their hands and knees on the worn wooden floor. They would climb up on his back, take hold of his suspenders and pull his hair; they would put a string between his teeth and be allowed to ride him piggyback to the middle of the room; they would make him whinny and force him to buck and, because he liked to act for everyone who clapped hands, he would throw over one or two chairs, miming a horse's fearless rage. Then, once the children were tired out and had fallen asleep on the couch, he would pick them up in his arms with great tenderness and put them to bed in the attic dormitory crowded with tiny white beds. It would no doubt be snowing outside, and there would be much smoke in the house; so many people would come to this party, and they would sing to become happy children again in the presence of their aged parents. (To jig to tunes that were old and almost forgotten, to be present only in the movement of your feet hitting the wood and to tell stories, surrounded by fat women with resonant laughter.) The table was set in the sunroom that smelled of hot meat pies and tobacco. The spittoons were gleaming beside the chairs, and before you, if you scratched the frosted windows, there was only a vast whiteness and the round moon in the sky. The sled's runners were sliding through the snow and masses of sweat were forming between the horses' legs as they trotted with their tails lifted up, their large anuses moving like pink flowers in the fur. The candle was burning slowly and wax was running over onto the paper Milienne had set on the draped orange crate. Milien had lit his pipe; the bowl felt warm between his fingers. He left Milienne sleeping and returned to the kitchen. The cat had fallen asleep again in Milienne's chair and the Old Man left it there. He walked to the window and played with the white string of the blind. Peace and silence enveloped the world, darkness had done away with those obstacles against which his thoughts might have stumbled. There remained nothing more to do, other than the act of looking that cancelled itself in the whiteness. The house creaked, the familiar sounds of winter were returning: it was the wind whistling under the doors and making the stove roar, its flames like the faces of Indians fighting strange battles. (It was also Mathilde's sobs and Milienne's snoring and the dog's chain and its howls rending the cold.) He had fallen asleep, his head between his hands, his eyes still full of the images seen in the room where Milienne must have closed her mouth by now. He had wakened with daybreak and taken some bread and greaves while the water boiled in the kettle. He understood that all night, in his sleep, he had been waiting for Milienne's liberating arrival. But the dream did not end. It burrowed into him and into his fatigue, so that he wasn't really hungry and he ate merely not to be cut off from the world of his habits. At around eight o'clock, he had finished all the bread and the entire bowl of greaves. "Are you coming, Milienne?" he called out. His voice broke at the other end of the kitchen and didn't reach the bedroom; he saw the words falling heavily to the floor. He didn't dare to speak anymore for fear of becoming aware that he was now unable to make sounds. He had never felt so worn out, as if all the autumn's labor, the ploughing, the uprooting and removal of stumps, the mountains of potatoes to be packed into sacks, was battering down on him and emptying him of all his energy. For the first time, the world of the house seemed hostile to him; evil forces began turning round the room, inhabiting it with a fear that veiled his eyes. "Maybe I ate too much?" he questioned himself. He burped several times and spat thick gobs of saliva, changed the brown ball of tobacco he had in his mouth and even tried singing. This new violence that was in his gestures and even in his thoughts terrorized him. (On the bridge leading to the hayloft the bull has already been struck several times on the skull with the mallet, but he does not fall. He remains motionless against the posts, his look filled with an accusing tenderness. Then the rifle rattles from being loaded quickly and there's the sound of the bullet smashing in under the eye. The bull falls heavily to the floor made of badly joined boards. Chien Chien Pichlotte takes the long white knife out of the sheath, tests the bull's neck and sinks the blade down into the big artery. The thick blood spurts out and stains Chien Chien's boots as he lights his pipe and throws the match into the blank eye. The bull's hind legs are solidly attached to the pulley, and this is the way he rises toward the big beam in the middle of the barn. Then the head is cut off in a pool of blood and he takes it by the horns and throws it near the manure heap. Then he and Chien Chien arm themselves with razor-sharp knives and skin the bull. His skin is like pie dough; you just have to give tiny jerks with the knife while holding the skin taut. Milien couldn't stop himself from touching the swollen organs, the yellow balls and the long member under the stomach. It still excites him a lot; this bleeding, neutralized virility increases his own by ten and makes it extraordinarily sensitive to the images that come to him while the snot rolls down from his nose and would freeze there if he didn't wipe his mouth with his parka. It feels good to walk in bull's blood while thinking that soon he will open its stomach with Chien Chien Pichlotte's knife and that its whole hidden life, hot and steaming, will suddenly come out along with the smells of blood and the excrement that makes brown stains along the intestine walls.) Milienne's groans filled the house like big sickly birds. (Noisy priests in an endless procession.) The Old Man took from the shelf a large Bible that Mathilde had given him; he began reading as he did every morning before going to work in the fields. He was particularly fond of the Book of Job; he could have been that old man — everything was possible on his land — next to the gigantic manure heap near the barn. Completely naked, scabby and dirty, he sits in the refuse with the old book open on his knees, and they come from far and wide to see his long white beard, his blind eyes and the demons that persist against him, tempting him and spitting with pleasure in his face to madden him. The floor creaked under the chair's runners; he breathed in the rotten smells coming from the spittoon which was like a misshapen hat near his feet. It was nine o'clock but Milienne still wasn't up. Outside the snowmobile was sliding fast through the snow, leaving great white clouds behind it. Hearing the dog's barks, Milien left his thoughts and forgot his fears. He lifted the door's latch and was swallowed up in darkness as he walked down the stairs. Only the green eyes glowed in the dark. The Old Man said: "Silence, dog; hey, silence." He put his hand on the collar and undid the buckle. The dog jumped. There was the sound of cans being turned over and the Old Man remained motionless, smelling the potatoes softening in the cellar. His eyes had a lot of trouble adjusting to the dark. In the cellar everything was hazy, shadows made black spirals where phantoms and monsters conjured up evil for Milienne. The Old Man sniffled, then stood up. He saw the dog under the table, licking the plate in which — (the big piece of red meat). Couldn't Milienne stop groaning in the bedroom? (The roosters have stopped singing since October; the yard is white, the fir trees are cones of snow, the Boisbouscache resembles a road trespassing into the forest's privacy. At Dubé's place, the pigs sleep in the living room and the rabbits dwindle away in the black cellar.) "Milienne," said the Old Man. "How come you're not up this morning?" The dog wanted to play with him. His legs were beating against the Old Man's thighs and the animal pretended to be biting his wrist. With his other hand Milien was pushing him away, but the dog was persistent. (Too many zigzags in the grass. The hole of a groundhog disembowled along the fence like a wound.) A gust of cold wind swept through the kitchen as he opened the door to let the dog out. He rubbed his hands together. "Milienne is dead," he thought. He took the poker from the box near the stove, and the flames danced wildly. (Under the heap of vegetables in the wet sawdust, the rats were burrowing secret paths, deep corridors at the end of which they would die of poisoning.) "Milienne is dead," he thought. These words were too vast — no image came from them — and even disquieting. Before the doorway, he said: "D'you know it's pretty late, Milienne dear?" Then he stepped foward. "Are you sleeping, Milienne?" Her eyes were wide open and staring at the dirty lightbulb on the ceiling. "My stomach hurts," she said. "It's like fire inside." He approached her and sat on the edge of the bed. "I'd rather be on my feet," she said. She wasn't in the habit of talking when lying down. Her voice rumbled like a river; it was full of menace, without tenderness, and painfully dry. It was as if during the night, it had risen from the deepest part of herself only to burst with the morning. "I can do that for you," he began. She had straightened herself up and her bun of hair had come undone. In her grey hair, in that disordered mass, there was still great strength. "I'll get up soon, I can't stay this way forever." He made no gesture toward her, he hardly even looked at her, and then he walked out of the room. The dog was barking on the doorstep. The Old Man let him in and then let himself be coaxed to play with him. He turned the dog over, then made him play dead, caressing him between the front paws to show that he was satisfied with him. (And the dog's penis stood up in the fur.) The Old Man kicked him and there was snarling and fangs at his ankle; then another kick, harder this time, and the dog let go of his leg and ran to hide behind the armchair. A few drops of blood were running down Milien's leg where the dog had sunk his teeth. "He's getting mean," said Milien, leaning against the bedroom door. "I'll have to get rid of him." He turned his head toward her. (What, had she toppled over?) There was Milienne, the same as ever, dragging her feet toward him. He was going to say: "I'm glad to see you come out of it safe and sound, Milienne," when she stumbled against the chair and fell heavily to the floor. (But: the heavy raft slid over the Boisbouscache waters, knocking against the reefs, catching itself on dead trees rotting in the whirlpools where the yellow foam whirled round furiously. The waters were carrying great blocks of ice that crumbled, knocking against each other. Between the two mountains, the river became a lake where nothing of the known world remained; the small islands that these structures made were dark stains, obstacles, growths that threatened the new order; the water's anger could do nothing against their strength and so it turned toward other places where it would reassemble its energy and follow the raft in the Boisbouscache's furious madness. It was night already. The moon was shining on the surface of the water that was like a thick veil thrown over things. Everything was indistinguishable; the country had slid into the chaos of spring and man's rebellion was hopeless, the sign that terror had taken hold of him. Crouched in the middle of the raft, the children were rolled up in woolen covers and Milienne was kneeling among them, praying for their salvation with her arms shaped in a cross. Only he remained standing. He had tied his wrists to the tiller and was looking solely toward the future which was awaiting them between the trees to complete its design.

The big yellow cat had bared its claws and the fur was standing straight up on its back; it was meowing with eyes like marbles of fear. Maybe the river's water had changed to blood? On a hillock a horse and three cows were watching them pass. Milienne said: "Florence is dead, Milien." She was holding the tiny girl to her breast, crying because of those bones that were crushed in broad daylight when Florence had innocently gone toward the Boisbouscache. She was swallowed up in the water along with her screams, and Milien had fished her from the eddies after too many thrusts of the raft against the blue flesh. The raft was going to disappear in the middle of the river, in the cold primitive back-country. The cat, after scraping through the log's bark, had already lost its claws and fallen into the river. "So, did everything end in the last winter frost?" . . . .

. . . .

. . . . "There, you've been beaten again," said Milien, throwing the deck of cards a last time on the table with a great burst of laughter. The Old Man sniffled. "I haven't the head for it today." He had the cards in his hands, but it was too much just to ask him to deal them to his friends. Something like shame took hold of him and fought against him in the inner darkness. Maybe we remain forever like

children tied to the present and the imme-
diate, and with no real knowledge of fear
but afraid all the same, as if at any moment,
deep down, some fabulous beast were waiting to threaten this tranquil assurance made
up of thousands of years of living, beginning with ourselves. Fear was as much in
the past as in the future, nothing was ever
really calm. There was always a great deal
of violence in these acts that were com-
mitted, in these planned gestures, even
those directed toward a breast when you
needed many hands to cover the nipple, and
great strength to lay the woman down on
the bed to couple with her. The world was
a tissue of hostile forces and man was a
bull's-eye upon it, exposed to every explosion of anger and, what was worse, to
the anger itself of merely being in the day-
to-day world. But the Old Man had no
memory of his childhood. Maybe that was
because he had never come out of it.
Perhaps it was only the habit of childhood that had tricked him and made him
believe that much time had passed since the
death of his father. Images came to him.
They were full of little white men running
through the streets of Saint-Jean-de-Dieu;
they were tiny, and yet they had long white
beards and sparse hair on their heads and
canes and ugly glasses and they lost their
wind quickly and had to hold onto picket

fences not to fall. And their daughters were even smaller than they were, misshapen-like under large polka-dotted dresses that were like mountains at the stomach — and the wrinkles, and the varicose veins, and the rotten teeth in their mouths. "Time for me to leave," said the Old Man. "I'd like to stop by Chien Chien Pichlotte's along the way." He got up after throwing his cards on the table. With the end of his cane he struck the lightbulb suspended from a cord on the ceiling. "If you want, I'll go with you," said the first Milien. "Me too," added the second. The Old Man put on his hat and passed his hand over his mustache. "O.K. W'e're leaving." Felt boots began to squeak loudly. It was the rain that had brought on so much humidity. Silently they walked side by side down Main Street, short and fat with their hair slicked back and the ritual armbands on their arms. They had come the same way and they only felt friendship for Chien Chien Pichlotte because he was crazy. And later, wearing a miter, the bishop would give them each a slap to rid them of the devil. The church would be filled with their own children who would sing for them in the choir. They would wear the white vest-ments and their faces would be transformed with emotion. The canticles would be said loudly so that the host could melt quickly in their mouths. It had been a long time since he had felt so good. All anger and sadness had vanished from him; the topsy-turvy world was trailing its delicate feet through the dusk. White vapor was rising over the Boisbouscache. So everything was fine as it was as the Old Man walked through a silent dream, not even aware that the Miliens had abandoned him, left him alone on Main Street to walk toward something that would be horrible and malicious. (Like the shapeless movement of earth in the dark. Like the tiny bitch being broken in by the big male, turning into a stream of warm blood behind the shed. Like those howls reaching the center of his being, making him twist in a pool of piss, broken there by his impotence and over-satiated desire. The big dog was running under the trees with the forest coming to meet him, drawing him into itself.) To continue on his path through the nightmare was difficult; Milien knocked on the door and entered without awaiting an answer. Maybe nothing would happen any more? Maybe, on the contrary, everything remained yet to happen? He saw his friend, Chien Chien Pichlotte, naked, and on all fours. Chien Chien Pichlotte had buckled the ritual leather collar round his neck and was tugging at the leash. Soon the room would be filled with growls. How come Chien

Chien's bites were not terrible weapons in the dark? "Shut up Chien Chien, shut up," said the Old Man. The beast bent his head, quieted down and folded his bandy limbs with knots of flesh at the elbows. Chien Chien Pichlotte stretched out before the Old Man's foot and his gaping mouth began to open and close. All the pain hidden in the world's heights descended into the incoherent sounds of this aged beast. "Do you act like a nut all the time?" the Old Man could have said while striking a match. He saw the lantern on the table, took off the glass-shade and lit the wick. "Lie down, Chien Chien, lie down." The smell of excrement heaped in a pile on newspaper sheets in a corner made him sick to his stomach. He opened the window. Chien Chien Pichlotte began to bark (the moon in the depths of the sky was like the stomach of a pregnant woman). The Old Man hadn't the time to say: "They're going to lock you up if you go on like that," for Chien Chien Pichlotte had leapt on him and bit his wrist. The Old Man forced him to let go by hitting his rump with a cane. Pichlotte went to hide under the table, covered his head with his hands and humped his back. His small tail stuck out between his bum, looking ridiculous. (This, no doubt, was how death came: the organs deflated, the penis shortened and weighed down between

the legs; the urine got blocked up somewhere in the stomach and then you had to
go to the hospital and get an earful of
the ambulance's red siren, and hands
touching your private parts, and the gossipy
orderlies bringing bottles, and the piss slowly coming down the tube pushed into
the penis and the transparent plastic bag
that looked like a sordid sticky animal lying
on its side.) "Chien Chien," said the Old
Man. And he sat down in the big broken
armchair with a hole in the middle like a
slack mouth hung open. Chien Chien
Pichlotte must have made the hole by biting
into the leather and springs. "So, Chien
Chien?" said the Old Man. But the animal
was sleeping, his head on his feet. The Old
Man began to sing. It was something with
an authentic tenderness and unbearable
agony, and the ears of the possessed dog
began moving while he stretched himself
like a monstrous cat with crooked fingers.
(So it was through sex that death finally
came: one day the penis tightened up in
the body and the warm odor of piss could
no longer be smelled except in the rotting
bowels.) The Old Man wiped the tears that
were running down his cheeks. He finally
said: "Chien Chien, why do you act like
a nut — eh?" For Chien Chien Pichlotte
was clawing through a pile of refuse with
his two front paws; dirt was falling on the

Old Man's boots and the dust made him sneeze. "Chien Chien, I'm going to brain you with my cane." He should have said this a long time ago: Chien Chien Pichlotte was getting mad and digging at the ground more and more violently. (All this had started one morning when Chien Chien Pichlotte refused to get up: "This morning I feel like staying in bed, I feel like opening my underwear flap and pissing hard. I want to wet my thighs, my hairs and my tiny asshole. It goddamn well belongs to me, doesn't it?" And he pissed good and hard: a big brown salty spray. Then he wanted to drink like a baby, sucking at the nipple of the warm milk bottle. He had put on an awful bonnet and he had got into the big cradle and, all curled up and naked, he let the milk run down the sides of his mouth. It was only after that he had violent convulsions, screaming of the lunacy that was taking hold of him in great epileptic fits of anger; he hurled himself against doors, broke window panes with his fists and the blood flowed from his wounds and he swallowed it greedily before rolling himself complacently in his faeces. His anus was a tumor between his buttocks that had become red, just like a baboon's ass. The long turds soiled his legs, blackened his hands, gave his mouth a strange obscene negroid grin. All of this remained still to be explained; it could only be a trap to keep the truth away, some kind of cancer issued from a televised image viewed too long in the dark before sleep which might have relieved him of it like a crippling deformity.) Only melted butter appeased Chien Chien Pichlotte. The Old Man made him swallow it from a tarnished spoon while patting his head, and the beast calmed down, closed his eyes and ended up by falling asleep with one finger in his mouth. (Without eyes he was a thing that could no longer be identified: an emaciated animal, or a son ravaged by fever, or oneself separated from oneself, cut off from the machine, cut off from the televised image reproduced thousands of times, cut off, cut off, cut off. In the end only this word could be said without lying.) The Old Man took Chien Chien Pichlotte in his arms and set him on the dirty bed from which a dreadful stench of filth was rising. After that, there was the washing of feet (the Old Man kneeling at the edge of the bed, opening Chien Chien's toes to clean out the filth, courageously wiping the hardened black soles and the skinny ankles that looked hairless and dried-up. He was Noah getting drunk and caressing the root of the vines. He hummed a song and spat into the basin. The small brown boats fought the waves and finally sank, caught under oceans where sea monsters would feed on their blood), and of Chien Chien's clothing: the old clothes that were black and dusty and could hardly be buttoned at the stomach, and then the long wait for death in darkness and silence. ("Sing," said Chien Chien Pichlotte. "You've got a beautiful voice and a good heart, and I love you because you understand me inside." He was sobbing and the breath that came from his mouth was rotten.) No doubt this violence was his only outlet for the pain, for Chien Chien's solitude turning like a dervish in agony. The light of the lamp was getting lower now that there remained hardly any oil. Dribble was running down the Old Man's chin while he dozed and thousands of big yellow cats ran between his feet meowing. "Oh Milien, the fire's in my stomach. Give me a bit of water." It was his fat wife lamenting now, her mouth only a tiny hole in her swollen face. "Put your hands on my navel. I'm leaving now. Pray for me Milien." The white storm was blowing outside and they were alone in the thick night, disintegrating, tumbled over inside the big diseased stomach. Chien Chien Pichlotte was holding his hand. "Stay with me. Stay, Milien, because my heart hurts no longer." (Was this called a dream?) Milien could no longer look at the beast; there was too much indecency in

this vicious body. So he took his cane, pulled his hat down over his head, waved goodbye to the good woman who led him to the door, thanking him for having come to console what nevertheless could no longer continue. The Old Man noticed the open bottle of pills in her hand. Above the door, in a frame of silver spangles, was Christ's bleeding heart with flames spurting from it and a dagger planted in the auricle. "I'm *tired,* lady!" he muttered. To say: "I've got to get back to the house," would that have been more effective? . . . .
. . . .
. . . .
. . . . .But nothing could have happened thus. Nothing could have been so simple. When the Old Man had left Main Street, his friends had already separated from him and slipped into the night that seemed endless as if it would be carried away in its own movement, in black chaos. There would be, from now on, only near-beings and forms and it was in this that the danger consisted: in what would become deformed forever. Negative time, the reverse side of the known world, would open itself. (We would become superstitious, carried away by obscene cults, at the mercy of barbaric massacres. Saint-Jean-de-Dieu would be filled with gypsy women, fortune tellers, naked sorcerers preaching great mutilation

100

rites, and there would be Dionysian sab-
baths perpetrated by old people. Sounds of
bells, magical xylophones, holy words filling their thick skulls. And maybe we will
finally be permitted to be incestuous and
sadistic and happy.) At the top of the knoll,
Chien Chien Pichlotte's house was lit up;
the bullfrogs were praying in the swamps
that would dry up when the country all too
soon burned and vanished in dust. The Old
Man knocked. (Who's there? — The
Happy Troubadours — Well, come on in!)
He pushed on the door's latch and was
blinded by several lightbulbs, glaring on the
room's ceiling. A one-room house, limit-
less, on the fringe of Saint-Jean-de-Dieu, no
doubt like a signal. What could there be
beyond it, if not the end of all that was
possible, if not murder or some terrible
settling of accounts? Everything became
laughable. To grow old had no meaning
because it was impossible to end false sit-
uations, because you constantly needed
descriptions, because it was stupid to
remain motionless to think of essential
ideas. The imagination was an evil power;
it made you waste time, it constituted one
of the terrible methods of getting lost.
The Old Man could not think that;
his imagination would not allow it; it
hurled him into the world of memories.
But maybe remembering was only creating

the present? Nothing had happened. Everything happened somewhere in absence, between the walls of the future and the past. The Old Man remained on the threshold of the door, deaf and silent, an old lump of white hairs and wrinkled flesh. It was this urge to piss that troubled him, reminding him still that he must not allow himself to be totally swallowed up by Milienne (she was urinating into the basin and the white recipient was a curse between her open legs, and the drops of piss ran down the crack (two nudges with the axe were enough to make that opening), and fell into the basin. Sometimes a drop got lost in the hairs or was stopped in the furrow. The Old Man took a cloth and wiped her rump. There was still no blood in her urine, that would come later when Milienne's huge body weakened. She would no longer move and he would spend his days and nights at her bedside. He would see life slowly leaving Milienne, slipping away from the fatty pads in her neck, her arms, her breasts, her stomach; only her buttocks would remain enormous, and her legs would be a vice in which he would no longer be smothered. She said: "If you only knew how I'm resting. I'm old, Milien. Old." She would not be ashamed of her nudity, nor of her infirmity; she could no longer pass judgment on that, her mind being occupied by other things altogether. Birds maybe, big white birds flying through the room. And warm shit (all that remained alive in her), was soiling the sheet. The Old Man turned her onto her stomach. She gritted her teeth not to scream, but it was so good to be at the mercy of powers which were beyond one's control — that in her pain there was joy. Milien was washing her ass, he couldn't stop himself; to massage the buttocks and wet the crack and smell, above all to smell the brown turds was a proof and a grace. "Milien, Milien," she stammered, biting the pillow. Maybe happiness was born of contradiction. Maybe all emotion was either a rape or a spurt of blood. Maybe now it had to stink and be ugly for there to be love or only some affection. One word was possible and this was the word Milien was saying as he looked at his wife's rosy bum: "Beautiful, beautiful, beautiful, beautiful"... and he was nothing now but an overly-stiff phallus. She had fallen asleep with the tip of her tongue between her teeth. He took the basin full of urine and went to empty it into the pot under the bed, but he could not resist his desire. To dip his fingers into the basin, wet them with piss, open his mouth and suck. The cow had humped her back and lifted her tail; the urine fell hard between the legs. Milien approached her after washing his hands. "Stay, Milien, stay. Your little woman is real sick." He seated himself and the floor creaked under the chair's runners; he was smoking his pipe and watching over Mathilde in the dormitory. He was watching over her because of her feverish eyes. He hardly found the time to spit a gob of brown saliva into the spittoon at his feet. (The world was silent, with no new faces henceforth.)

. . . .
. . . .
. . . .
. . . ."Well, come in Milien." The Old Man walked toward Chien Chien Pichlotte. He saw only the head of his friend who was lying in bed — a portion of yellow skin and sunken eyes. Chien Chien Pichlotte drew out his hand and gave it to him to shake. The palm was clammy and the Old Man held it firm and close for a long time. "Do you know that I'm going to die?" Without a denture in his mouth, how could a man be recognized? The Old Man said: "I can't stay very long tonight." The hand crept under the covers. "Me neither, Milien." It was so easy to destroy a man that Milien turned his eyes away. The whole room was a repulsive pen. Too much dust, too many empty bottles under the bed, too many things rotting and too much vermin: death could not really come,

it would get caught in the spider webs. "I'm feeling real low," said Chien Chien Pichlotte. He straightened himself up a little. To look no longer at that neck and that gullet like a tumor under his chin, and that emaciated face showing clearly what would come soon: so nothing could really be attempted; and did one absolutely have to witness all this? The Old Man was suddenly afraid and terrorized. He stammered: "Give me time," and then he understood all the weakness of his despair and the ridicule of his defense: what had he come here to do tonight? Was Saint-Jean-de-Dieu so small that death could take hold of it entirely? "Speak to me, Milien. You've got to speak to me. It's as if I've heard nothing for years." So he had to open his mouth and contrive another description for his friend to whom he had just given a drink. "Do you remember our Trip — do you?" Chien Chien Pichlotte rocked his head and his eyes grew large. (There was something not right there which the Old Man could not identify. Nothing could have any consequences now and nothing could be said to bring the old world back to them, and nothing should be attempted to return to its origins as Milien was trying to now. He was conscious of the dimensions of the lie he would have to perpetrate, and he could not add a word. Too many images were suddenly invading him: the Trip was losing its privileged meaning and was becoming something obscure which possibly had never happened, or which had been tried under circumstances too banal to be truthful. It would have been better to have died before everyone else. To be the first placed into the big crate, *that* was an act belonging only to the father. Instead they had all fallen before him, even if they had no white hair, nor a long curling beard, nor twisted legs. What memory could be effective against that? And here he now had to speak of events that accused only the members of his tribe. It was still too early for this idea, which he was denying, to come to him; he simply felt like crying.) "Talk to me about the Trip," Chien Chien Pichlotte moaned. "You're the only one who can do it." The Old Man said: "O.K.," and he began the tale. It was two years before a War. He had just bought an enormous car and now he had to go into the great world to rebuild his clan which was threatened by distance. While Milien and the kids saw to it that the real frontiers of the known world did not budge in his absence, he and Chien Chien, he and the two Miliens would climb into the big car, making the doors slam. (You had to get used to this new sound, entering a sound-filled world. The groans of the motor while changing gears, the friction of the brakes, the rumbling of the muffler, the scraping of windshield wipers, the rain on the hood; the car was an animal that would disfigure the landscape, accelerating the speed of images coming at you. Everything the eye saw would be dressed up in some alarming meaning, as if the mind were being filled with stains. Trees would no longer quite be trees and they would be something more than trees; everything would become confused; after seeing, you had to recreate decomposed things. And it was in the car that, for the first time, he would have the impression of being in a motionless stomach. You had only to lean your head against the back of the seat, close your eyes, and then it became immediately evident: we were foetuses, unformed flesh, we were nothing yet, but it felt so good in the big car and you had only to smell the first crushed cigarette butts in the ashtray in the front seat.) "What are you saying, Milien? You don't talk loud enough, I can't hear you so good." The Old Man opened his eyes; you had to be in the dark to speak well and to be perfectly understood. He said: "I'd like the lights turned off." Chien Chien Pichlotte said: "Don't be shy, Milien." The Old Man rose and walked to the light switch. He lifted his hand and everything disappeared in blackness. He felt relieved.

Now he could talk for hours, seated in a chair next to his old friend who remained silent except when he pissed into the bottle that Milien held out for him. Thus the long banal tale began again: it was only a question of everyday things and the Old Man put no warmth into it; the events told were either above or beneath emotion. He had to speak of dusty roads, numerous flat tires and the noisy farts of the two Miliens seated next to each other, smoking big cigars and laughing at the jokes they were making while the big car ate up space. Maybe they would never come back, they would get lost in the winding roads of the earth and wander through the depths of forests, and the car would become their home; it would never be able to stop anymore, carried off by its own momentum. They would have to cut a hole in the hood, make a small makeshift chimney and eat poorly-cooked meat. It was Chien Chien Pichlotte who was dreaming like this to break the monotony of the road. ("And me, I was thinking. I was thinking of my animals, and picket fences, and stakes piled up behind the house, and oats, and Milienne too. And I was saying to myself; 'All that will no longer be there when we come back. There will be neither houses nor animals nor children nor a woman to greet me. Trees will have overgrown the entire countryside while I was not there.' And yet they will all be with me, all the sons who had left home; I will have convinced them all to come back, and the same with the girls, and we will all be forever together at last. And then me, in my own time, I will be able to go.'') You had only to open your mouth and say these things so that nothing would appear menacing. Talking spoilt the event, limited your thinking, uprooted the violence of words and rarely allowed nightmares. (But the big car has already been travelling over unknown roads for many days. The farther you get away from Saint-Jean-de-Dieu, the more the things left behind you become hazy. Milienne suddenly no longer has a face; it lengthens, stretches out, gets bigger, becomes a ball of flesh, an ugly yellow lump, and then loses its eyes, mouth and ears; only the chin becomes larger and divides into ten other chins. This is the final victory of fat, the world having become an immense pocket of lard beneath the eyes; was this then the goal of the Trip and its most profound meaning? "Hey boys, why don't we all go back home?" It was too late. Now you had to go to the end and lose whatever remained of the known world and forget everything not to have to return empty-handed. (There would remain only the unchanging image of the edge of his

land, and the stream, and the white world.)
On the outskirts of the Great Morial, the
two Miliens became euphoric, as if all the
fatigue accumulated along the road, as if the
great quantities of alcohol drunk and the
belching, the heavy indigestible food, the
tiny space for your feet, the numbness,
the pins and needles in your thighs, the
uneasy sleep, the smoke, the chewing
tobacco between your teeth, the anony-
mous landscapes, the engine breakdowns,
as if all that could be forgotten only with
exuberance. The important thing to remember was movement; it was this movement that drew you ahead endlessly, as
if behind you there remained only fear. They
were running away with good reason, no
doubt; the back country was now only
drought or burnt woods. Only Chien Chien
Pichlotte remained calm; he had been sick
for nearly the whole trip, hiccuping and
vomiting, with his head stuck through the
door window. You would've thought he
was a tired-out dog with no longer the
strength to bark, and barely enough strength
to open its jaws and utter a few pitiable
groans. Also, he got hard slaps on the back
along with "Come on, Chien Chien, come
on." The city lay before them and they had
to sing, for once the bridge had been crossed there would be too many things luring
them on. The two Miliens were standing

on the running boards and they waved, their hats turning in circles at the end of their arms. The big car had slowed down on the bridge, there was no longer anything but water and huge buildings before them. ("Damn it, I love that," said one of the Miliens.) The Old Man was thinking of the mission's goal, the reunion he would soon call to order. He saw cars lined up in the middle of the city, old trucks filled with goods, his sons and daughters surrounding him, and the flow of children he had never seen before and who were the extension of his flesh in renewed forms. "It's too bad we don't have a fatted calf," one of his sons would say before the cars started. Yes, they would have to share and drink and eat much before returning to the known world. Otherwise, nothing would have happened. Maybe he had slept for too long. Chien Chien Pichlotte was moaning in the dark. His hands were jerking under the covers. "You're not fifteen anymore, with your hands on it all the time." Chien Chien Pichlotte did not answer. He held his breath and tried to keep still, but he was no longer the master of his hands. A big beautiful black bitch was running through his head. She was warm and welcoming, you just had to bark a little and go find her under the doorstep to forget your sickness. He would have liked to stay on her a long time, biting her ear, moving his behind and pumping his seed into the bitch's ass-hole in strong spurts. (And to free himself at last.) Once again there was the bottle of piss Milien held out to Chien Chien Pichlotte. He pissed into the bottle and there was also disease in his cock. Hardly any opening, only scabs of dry pus in the orifice. He was crying, it hurt so much to die from below. His heart was beating in his stomach. "Don't leave," he said. "Don't leave. I don't want you to leave." So he stayed, but kept silent. For a moment he no longer knew why he had come. To lie so much sickened him, he felt like he was drowning; nothing could happen any longer because they'd waited for it too long. He might just as well stay all night and go on with his story about the Trip — *that* could no longer calm down or deceive anyone. Kill. But which of his sons did he call Bouscotte? Which one had loved him enough to become violent and give him two black eyes? That happened at the edge of his land. He had quarrelled with his son for no reason. There was some kind of violence between them that had to be brought out. "Bouscotte," he thought. He did not want to fight him, for that would free forever the evil forces that were so deep in his nature. But it was sometimes difficult to avoid things and a refusal could not be sustained in certain distressing circumstances. Both of them had eaten and were seated face to face, having planted their axes into the spruce stump. They had said nothing. You had to see this agreement of silence as they swallowed their bread and crackling. His son sweated a lot, bit his lips and wiped his forehead with a great red-checkered handkerchief. And he himself was watching him. He felt admiration for this manly virility which was draining from his own body now at the start of his old age; the pain in his legs was bothering him as it told him that in a little while he would become in a way his son's son, which is to say a kind of big child who would be calm or capricious, who would have to be protected and made to eat perhaps, and led to church and undressed at night before being put to bed. That did not seem so hard for him to accept. His fear did not come from that; it came rather from his very own son, from behind those small eyes that looked upon him with violence. He had said: "Bouscotte," and that word alone had been enough. His son got up, furious and threatening, and his two fists battered down into his face. That's all that happened, nothing more had been said. There was a taste of blood in his mouth and the trees were twisted shapes in his eyes. He had fallen into the broken branches and was swallowed by the earth's *milky body*. He had needed the whole day to come back to himself and forget the blood that had dried on his face. He took the road back to the house in the night, worn out like he'd never be again and worried because he did not understand the meaning of what had just happened. Everyone was asleep in the house when he pushed open the door and then drank a big glass of water from the bucket on the cupboard. Everyone was asleep, except for Milienne who was seated in the chair and looking at him with her blank eyes. The opposite of his son. His negation. There could no longer be any question of maternity, Milienne would no longer menstruate. She would become the absence of womanhood, the imposing presence of some nameless and faceless thing that would make him understand he was no longer a man but the servitude of a man from which he'd escape only by breaking this new order his son's fists had established. Milienne had said: "He's no longer with us in our house." After saying that, she rose and went to bed. (She would no longer wholly be with him from now on.) So for a moment, the two Miliens, Chien Chien Pichlotte and the Old Man, were at the heart of their Trip; he had to walk through the Grand Morial, visit his sons, drink a lot, talk, talk, talk to hasten their return, to convince them. "But what do you want us to do in Saint-Jean-de-Dieu? The future is on our side, father. Stay with us." How could his sons understand what he himself barely knew yet? How could his sons guess that it was his persistence he wanted to save? Was the Father's need so strange to them? "My sons, my sons," he said to them, "this is our only chance to be." They made him drink so that he might forget the meaning of the words, and they gave great parties to trick him and they believed it was only the liquor that made him cry. And the woman whom he was intimate with in the midst of an outburst that did not come from him but from his sons who had suddenly grown weary of his monotonous demand. They had paid the two Miliens so that he might become in a night's time the black demon of a bought woman. His sons knew that after that, after having kissed her lips, caressed her breasts, patted her buttocks, lain on top of this woman and spurted his seed into her, he would not dare to appear before them again. They had killed him, they had destroyed the Father image. What remained to be done after that? Could he reasonably let himself be driven in the big car to Lowell where his last son was presumably happy in the new world? He knew that there was no longer any feasible plan, that by drawing farther away from Saint-Jean-de-Dieu he would merely advance this work of destruction. Once he'd reached the end of the road, there would no longer be any acceptable return, neither for his sons who had used forgetfulness so much for their existence, nor for himself who had fought it all his life. So he didn't return to see the children. He sold the big car, forgot Chien Chien Pichlotte in a tavern, quarrelled with the two Miliens, boarded a train and returned to Saint-Jean-de-Dieu. It was time to come back to the milk cans, the calves being born in the barn, the bleating sheep, the manure heap, the pots of excrement, the sound of long grass, the curtain of trees along the Boisbouscache, the white rabbits hopping in their dirty cages, the broken branches, the cows' piss, the stallion, the cats. Whatever died here died only a false death. Whatever died here could not really be touched, mutilated, detested, hated or beaten. As he no longer had any children and only Milienne was left to him, swollen with a diseased life (they would finish by taking away his Milienne), he would remain alone on earth and he would become old, his hairs as white as those of the world and his beard grown long and his legs hardly hurting him anymore. He would pull the big chair up to the window and sit, facing

116

the road on which he'd await the return of all that had made up his life thus far. ("Hey, Milien, are you sleeping?") For a moment, he no longer knew where he was; sleep had overtaken him right in the middle of a sentence, and it took him some time to find his words again. His throat was dry, his head hurt and he ignored all that had risen in him which was so absurd, so small and which had so suddenly put him in agony to the point where everything in him was now broken and silenced; perhaps he had fallen on the ground and slipped down into the Boisboustache River, which was the sign that all would die, for the water said clearly that nothing could be withheld and that not even death had a bed to lie in. "I can't move," he thought. "Am I paralysed?" He tried to move, but the muscles did not respond anymore: only fear lived within him, crouched inside his bones. "Milien, Milien, where are you, Milien?" He heard Chien Chien Pichlotte's voice. To tell the truth they were not words penetrating his ears, but arrows boring into his head. He was only trying to get up, gripping the chair that had tumbled over beside Chien Chien Pichlotte's bed, but none of that was possible anymore: he was dying at last. "Milien, Milien, where are you? Speak, speak Milien, speak to me." There was the sound of covers being thrown back; Chien Chien Pichlotte, an old battered skeleton, rises. His bones creak just like the floor. He knocks his foot against a beer bottle that rolls and stops at the end of its course. Then the weight of a hand on his forehead. They were undoing his necktie, opening his shirt; someone was massaging his heart, and this is how he fell back to sleep with his tongue between his lips, dribbling, all smiles, happy because of the flood of crazy thoughts invading him. He had never believed that, an orgy. An orgy! It was evil and he had always been a good man for whom everything, every word, every act, had to be a campaign for goodness. And here, now, at the moment of his departure, he was content because wicked thoughts were coming to him: in his dream he murders Milienne and all his children. Here he is running toward the barn where he will look for the double-edged axe. It's night, pitch black. Everything is still, like a prisoner of silence and the fresh smells that rise from the ground, making him sneeze, but soundlessly, for Milien had pinched his nose and everything was muffled in his mouth. It seemed to him that he had never been so big as that night; the idea of killing his family so that he might be the only one with some chance of surviving eternally, is not yet very clear to him; but it comes from far down inside him and nothing now can repress his desire. So he takes the axe and returns to the house, silently, bootless, so as not to make any noise, and without clothes, so that the blood (the spurts of pink liquid) would gush only over his skin, touching his hairs and his flesh to assure his immortality. First he climbs up to the dormitory in the loft where his nine children are sleeping, and pulls off the cover that hides his first son, and the axe, so light in his hands, whistles down and falls on the head. He is flooded with blood; it's warm, thick, invigorating. Once he's finished chopping the nine heads off, he pulls the bodies by their feet to the center of the dormitory and makes a little pyramid with the disfigured heads and sits in the blood. Something rises within him, an extraordinary feeling of joy that gives him great pangs in the stomach. He is like this, right in the middle of his joy, when Milienne climbs up the stairs; he hears her steps and the short sound of her breathing. It is dark, but he sees her perfectly in her white jacket; she has never looked so fat and so terrifying. He rises and says a few disjointed words, then Milienne advances, enveloped in a wicked silence. There is nothing in her face, no mouth, no eyes, she is like some kind of nameless deformity he must put an end to. He draws away from

her a little to let her pass; she walks up to the pile of corpses, lies over her children and begins to weep because she understands now that the axe has taken them from her forever. She embraces the blood, the arms that are under her, the chopped necks, the open eyes staring at the vision of the axe slicing the air. Naked beside her, he looks at her: why did she provoke him with her overly-big buttocks? He undresses her. Oh, no longer to see those milky breasts dragging so obscenely in the blood. He slips her jacket over her head — she is a big blind cow bellowing on a pile of refuse. The axe rises, rises in the black sky, making flashing whirlwinds. He misses his mark, shattering only the shoulder. The axe must strike again and again on the big body, bloody and broken, whose crushed bones.......................................
....
....
....
...........(And to finish with a boisterous laugh that lights up the sky, and to bathe Milienne's buttocks in lots of blood).......
....
....
....
.......Chien Chien Pichlotte was snoring when Milien awoke, his neck hurting from leaning against the back of the chair for

too long. He massaged the nape of his neck, gazed into the shadows in the face of his old friend; he looked like a potato all shrivelled up and soft, that would sprout badly because the sun was weak, making pale streams through the cracks in the rocks. You had to forget so many things so you could die, leave before the dawn in that agony that comes before the void. His nose was especially pitiable. Only the mouth remained beautiful, voluptuous still and covered with feminine marks and swollen with blood. Milien stood up and guided himself with his cane in the darkness; he walked on tiptoe like a dark bird who no longer had any feathers to unfold. The door hardly creaked, but that was enough to wake up his friend bundled-up stiffly in the bed. He lifted his hand; there was something so frightening about his emaciated arm (an old deformed penis, scaled, with veins like underground rivers) that Milien stopped the movement he was making to open the door. This hand stayed everything, stopped the world from turning; it was the presence of a repressive, unhealthy divinity. "So then, you're leaving?" He didn't answer. He removed the latch and was suddenly swallowed up by the cold night air. Once outside, the possibility of Chien Chien Pichlotte's death left him indifferent, as if his friend's final gesture had struck him with its absurdity, letting anger descend into him which could not be neutralized except through indifference. He walked in the road, between the big trees. There was nothing in the night but aspen leaves. Milienne had left at the break of day. They came for her in a green car. She had packed all her things into two big cardboard valises and here now the dust, lifted up in the air by the automobile, was falling over the bushes beside the road. He had said to her: "Go see your children, you should, Milienne. Trips are good when you want to get rid of sickness." The big body compressed into the light dress, the imposing muscles on her calves, the thick shoes deforming her legs, breaking her step so that it now resembled that of a ridiculous animal. She had laughed a lot before leaving, and it was possibly because of this laugh, and the beautiful mouth opening over her teeth, and those eyes that looked forgotten beneath the flesh, and those wisps of silver hair at her temples, and her heavy hand mopping her brow at each moment, that he was content to see her go. He had squeezed her arms, leaving red marks on her biceps, but he did not kiss her. There was too much dignity in the mouth and too much joyful strength in the movement of the jaws; kissing her would have felt like causing damage, breaking her teeth, mutilating her mouth as surely as if he'd raised his fist to her. These connections were mysterious to him, and confusing. They belonged no doubt to what was growing old and refusing, having consumed too much time, to let itself be encircled, enveloped, clamped down or outraged in some privileged moment. There is perhaps an age at which speech and action are impossible. Having lived a long time, we become incapable of living. We were chained too much to a past that has molded itself perfectly to the shapes of our body and spirit, so that it might appear improper to laugh or sing or again to undress your woman, to mount her and grunt forcefully in the obscene crack. So a moment came when an overabundance of the past constituted a barrier for living in the future. Old, you became so vulnerable and so tempted by the exterior event that, because it made for great absence of mind, deformed the world and projected it into a new aura, a new hardness from which you were never freed except by looking even more intently upon the salvation of everyday life, that everyday life packed full of lies. (Deep down, his woman's absence had not been so tragic: all he had to do was to go on doing what had to be done to avoid the explosion of emotions, no longer to be afraid of annihilating oneself in someone else's death. The cart rattled along the dirt road, its wheels scraping stones and making ephemeral furrows in water puddles. The world was filled with song. Long birds were gliding before his eyes which had become extraordinarily sensitive, and the cows were grazing on the hill in the peaceful dawn. Only their tails were swishing in circles, which was not enough to keep away the big blackflies that glued themselves to their skin to suck their blood. His two naked feet pressed against the stallion's backside, Milien was smoking; his soft penis, being tossed about by the cart's motion, was slowly becoming longer and little by little filling the space in his pants. That felt good and integrated itself into the world's peaceful sensuality. Only the temptation to shove his foot into the horse's anus disturbed the party for a moment. Milien put his boots back on; the stallion's ass was warm, the short black hair was shiny, and there was something noble in the way the tail was held up just slightly). Milienne was far, very far from all that. She must have reached the end of her Trip. He saw her strolling through the long streets where her grown-up children lived in alarming dispersion; she was walking with Mathilde, licking an ice-cream cone and saying banal things about a banal world. (This could no longer be a story, hardly a rape from which the pain would finally exclude itself when time, tired of her swollen stomach, would let herself go adrift. So there was no disquieting motive despite what the facts dictated. Nothing had happened except in the mind of someone who sat motionless before a cold cup of coffee, a dated book before his eyes. And why, finally, did he have to write of the Miliens in some far off place and of a fat woman sitting majestically on her piss pot?) The stallion was trotting, making the sacks of oats bounce in the cart. There were fields and trees beyond sight and nothing in the country could exist but in solitude. The important thing was to win the landscape over to one's cause, to tame the animals that were sliding sensuously through the ponds, or running over picket fences, or following obscure trails in the night into the heart of the forest, into some warm hole where the lazy female lifts her tail to ease coupling. Animals would always be in heat — that alone could not be changed, and everything else was commentary. Maybe Milien had never known how to love his woman, having too often preferred instead the pigs wallowing in the dirt, greedily eating the swill he emptied by the bucketful into the steaming troughs. Maybe he had even loved her too much and had done everything for her in those beautiful bursts of tenderness when the black night was falling fast and the rain sang on the iron roof and their first children were snoring in the dormitory beds, wrapped-up bundles of flesh, their toes dirty from running through warm cow-dung. He was thinking of that and of many other things while he let himself be taken to the village by his beautiful stallion. He was whistling, satisfied with the world, content to be only this old man who felt fine in the heat, seated on sacks of oats. He could have kept the instant and made it speak a long time, but he didn't need his memory at all; the cart was running well, the sun was like a soothing hand on his bare head, the word *police* sparkled beautifully on his big suspenders, and the blood in his feet had calmed down now that he had undone the laces: nothing better could happen, except for sleep perhaps and a few dusty berries picked up along the roadside. Raindrops were falling and the wind had risen; the entire sky was filled with the haunting sound of an airplane motor. Milien walked faster. He had already forgotten his old friend and everything that had happened till now. He was hungry and the poorly-digested gin was rising in his stomach and disintegrating into sickening smells once it reached his mouth. He bent over, closed his fists, picked up some blades of grass and brought them to his mouth. He chewed, spat, swallowed. He had become the brown stallion, some imposing lump of flesh galloping through Saint-Jean-de-Dieu. Everything told him that he must not go home; he should get away from the houses with pointed roofs which, seen from the hilltop, were like animals lying in a circle. So he walked aimlessly through the streets, thinking of nothing in particular, at the whim of what his eyes saw and of the rain which was now falling harder. Dogs were barking under doorsteps, catfights were going on in the fields. He saw pairs of phosphorescent eyes, a big tomcat jumped out from an underbrush and leaped onto the road; it was furious and hostile, hissing with rage, its tail drawing snakes in the grass. (So it was not always easy to be a cat; all you needed was a female with bad intentions, or a capricious one, or a better-equipped tomcat that could meow more vigorously and claw less cautiously, and then misfortune came and a heavy feeling of frustration barred your way.) There was a bench near the church; Milien let himself drop. He was tired, his lungs hurt. He thought of hoar-frost, of a huge icy pipe through which he was crawling, protecting his head with his hands so as not to be hit by the stalagmites. He suffered, but he did not know from where this suffering came and what space it occupied in his body and why it suddenly burdened him so much. No doubt some gesture had not been made at the right moment. Or else it was a word that, not having come from himself, disturbed the world's harmony, making within him a bottomless hole into which everything escaped in great pain. He took off his hat and shook it. Water fell onto the asphalt (drops of sperm that were too thin, inefficient, foul-smelling, old and rotten from having stayed so long in the limp penis). He would have wanted Mathilde to be there at his side; he would have liked someone from his family to say some words to him, anything; that wasn't what mattered, for everything was already in the familiar voice, and the words were said only to ease the presence of something more confusing that was being freed along with speech. But Mathilde was dead. They had put her body in the ground a long time ago and nothing human was recognizable in her anymore. So he had loved for nothing, stayed up late at night and had nightmares when his children called out to him for his protection, and worked without sparing himself, happy because the house was full of snotty, dirty *bouscottes* whom he took on his knees and for whom he sang gospel songs. They twisted his nose, put fingers in his mouth, shoved crayons into his ears, pulled at his mustache. All that ended in either big or little boxes, their interiors covered with red satin. And now in the rainy night, he was helpless, emptied, as if nothing had taken place; he had just been born in this old body and his punishment consisted in making efforts to remember: what baby would let itself be taken; into whose pink chubby flesh would he penetrate for the past to take up its place again and give him somewhere to grow? He was sad and yet he was smiling; there were events that remained forever, that he needn't recall if he wanted to stay in touch with himself. This was Milienne's trouble. She was unreachable other than through her disease. She came back from her Trip in an ambulance. She no longer spoke, except with her stomach which was extremely big and full of hoarse sounds whose harshness seemed offensive somehow. Two men had taken the stretcher out of the white car. He saw only her head, her open eyes staring at the sky, her mouth half-open and the thick wad of hair. He was on the doorstep looking at the stretcher coming up toward him. He swallowed a lot of saliva and bit into his lip: this woman had died far from him, in the boredom of the Trip, between two callous stretcher-bearers, in an ambulance racing full speed down the road. They carefully slipped her into bed; she was crying, holding her stomach, ashamed of suffering so much and being no longer able to hide it. And he himself, what else could he do but remain motionless at her side, his eyes filled with tears, for wasn't this his woman who was leaving? And more than his woman? "Don't stay, Milien. Go back into the kitchen, Milien dear. Leave me. I don't want you to see this." No, that he could not do, to keep a vigil was his duty, and that's all that counted. She made such efforts not to writhe, not to upset the strong, quieting image he had of her. "Leave Milien, oh leave," she wept. He took her hand, she was all cold now, her flesh marbled with great stains and pockets of fat had swelled up all over her body. And outside, the dog was howling, seated on its back paws with its tail in cold turds. (After that, the world became silent. He had destroyed the world's frontiers, turned over the milk buckets facing the dairy, scattered the haycocks in the fields, flooded the Boisbouscache, frightened the animals that were bucking, thrust horns into himself, all amid the racket of chains and yokes rattling. The chickens were fleeing with their stumplike wings spread out and their small yellow feet splashing in the mud. Only the pigs had not moved yet, sitting pretty in their excrement, the piglets gnawing awk-wardly at the dirty teats. The house was moving; it was a ploughshare opening the soil to deposit the swellings that fell from Milienne's body.) He had seated himself in the kitchen and was rocking. His shadow looked grotesque on the wall. He had taken his pipe and the tobacco pouch made from a pig's bladder, filled it, drawn a match from the box and lifted his leg; the spark exploded, he was holding the match with his fingertips, listening to Milienne groan-ing in her agony. The flame was burning his skin, but he remained motionless, unable to suffer other than in his woman's screams. Then he rose, went into the bed-room and ran toward Milienne who, with eyes rolled up, was no longer able to wet her cracked lips with her tongue. He trembled from an overabundance of use-less energy, as if his body attracted every-thing in the room which still might have been of some use to his woman. At least he would not have wanted a hard-on, but his cock was completely rigid, erect in his pants like a provoking demon. He walked out of the room and left Milienne to battle with death while he, before the window, put his hand into his pants and began mechanically caressing the pouch, big like a tiny pumpkin between his legs. He didn't want to do evil, but he knew that with the

end of his erection Milienne's life would also end. So he was keeping the fire in the pouch, completely despairing, ashamed and unable to think. The world was gorging itself with water; the fir trees were too green in the night; you would have thought that everything was turning upside down and that your head was where your feet ought to be and your stomach was falling down, dripping into your mouth. He was going to vomit in the sink and look at the refuse his body had thrown up. (But we must return to the bench, to the hard rain and the Old Man who was soaked, trying to get a match lit to fire up his pipe. He didn't dare get up. He was cold and hungry; he was terribly tired and terrorized. He finished by dropping his pipe into a pool of water and when he bent over to pick it up, everything broke inside him: his muscles became lax, his eyes no longer saw anything and he slipped from the bench, shivering and afraid. He was going to die in hideous solitude and would not know what was to happen to his body. He opened his mouth to tell the world of his fate, but only swarms of toads and fishworms came out and fell into the water, crawling through the mud, hopping grotesquely with their deformed legs and bodies) . . . .
. . . .
. . . .

. . . . .He must have wakened once the nightmare came to an end. Then he rose. He was blind and sounds were ringing in his ears with such force that he put his two wet hands over them. How had he been able to drink so much and empty the big gin containers so quickly? That was a mystery and could not be explained. Now he had to go home at all costs; someone was dying in his house and still needed him to be able to leave in the proper tradition. He leaned on the bench. His head was an echo chamber amplifying every sound, and when he spoke, he failed to recognize his voice that was like cracked glass. A hearse had parked before the church, cars covered with flowers were arriving; he heard doors slam; everything must be dark, impossible to look at. It was Mathilde's body they were wheeling into the church, it was her bronze coffin they were covering with a black sheet and setting four big candlesticks around. He began to sing as the death ritual demanded and the water was now every-where in him, in his eyes as well as his feet. He no longer had a choice from now on; nothing could be done so long as he failed to return to that house which was not his and where a woman whom he would not recognize was dying. That woman had never been anything but shame in his thoughts, an obscure vile stain, a dull presence against which his whole mind had leagued itself with no other motive than the refusal to die alone. (It was this dryness in Milienne that had broken everything within him, a coldness she set between herself and the rest of the world, silences that allowed nothing but wounds which could only be healed with indifference or anger. Now he would have liked to finish in peace, reading that old Bible Mathilde had given him and thinking of the past, of animals, crops, soap being made in the vats and of numerous events that had happened too quickly to go far into them and empty them of all their substance and so be wholly freed of them; he had only begun thinking of all that, and from the depths of his being came signs which he could not identify because Milienne was calling him, waging a subtle silent war with him that he could only lose because he did not want to use his strength and he refused to change. His remarrying had been a childish gesture made in a moment of foolishness and dependance while there came to him, with overwhelming strength, images preceding Milienne's death. He had wanted to be in familiar surroundings and to make gestures again that had been made so many times with such intensity: to place his dirty hand on Milienne's fat neck, to look through a half-open door at the efforts of a woman

134

whose dress, lifted to the knees, was a veil under which a world of disturbing smells was moving like a pack of wild animals, and to bite the pads of flesh on her hips and penetrate deep into her navel, and to walk on tiptoe in the morning, leaving the house to go to the animals bellowing in the yard, and to see the rosary slowly mesh through her heavy hands while her lips moved and, and, and, and so much sweetness, such calm passion whose silence was but one expression of its appropriation. So much tenderness that did not strive to be expressed, which was brutal like the country, and Milienne understood it and amplified it with her respectful attitude. And he had thought that another Milienne would make it all possible again, allowing him to go even farther with gestures that were more practiced, to which she would consent with a joy that would finally transform his face, his body and even his thoughts. Instead, she destroyed everything and replaced the images of former times with a hostility that annihilated all transformation. (Emptiness.) It was no doubt because of the cats that she detested him the most; she did not accept him giving them such special attention, rocking them, and speaking to them while they stretched out against his legs, purring, with yellow eyes staring at the stains the sun made in the window. When he returned, the cats would have fled the house; they would no doubt be dead, shamefully killed, their skulls bashed in with the spade. Milienne's fits of anger were terrible, but in a sense he loved her more when she was angry, for all the uncertainties ceased then and the ambiguity of their relationship vanished, leaving room for an intimate world charged with evil. Milienne was a witch and it wasn't for nothing that, raving against him, he imagined her wearing a long pointed hat and riding an enormous broom. "You are only an old fool," he had said to her once. This was the one indulgence he had ever permitted himself; he did not want to fight her, not having the time: "Milienne dear, I wanted to talk to you, I just wanted to talk, but, great God, I see now that you've never had any ears!" He saw her motionless before the sink, her hands splashing in the water. She was stubborn, hard-headed, refusing to answer him as if washing the dishes was a justification for everything; or as if she'd acted out some mediocre comedy behind his back and the same dull scene had to be repeated again and again till it suddenly became heavy and grotesque. He himself looked at her and went on rocking his chair, his two feet resting on the runners. All he needed were the reins in his hands for the stallion to come back onto the road, running in all its majesty. "That old fool," he said to himself, thinking of possible ways to outrage his woman. He stood up, walked behind her, slipped her dress over her head, removed her yellow panties and, kneeling, he did in broad daylight what he had only once before permitted himself to do to Milienne; he was mistreating her, but it was by doing evil that their potential goodness realized itself. Maybe he had been too calm, had let himself become too tender. His mistake was that he had never been the master, he had permitted defiance to come between them. Oh, there were things that could not be forgotten! Unhappy words that stayed in his memory and would make for a terrible weapon at the ultimate moment. Thus Milienne had said one day, after opening the door and rushing in before the strangers who had come from the great and distant Morial to pray with Milien over Mathilde's body: "Hey, you people, do you know that this isn't his house. This is my house, see. All this, it's mine, mine; do you know that?" She repeated this sentence all afternoon with a chilling monotony that ruled out any other words. The strangers were ill at ease and ate only sugar creams in the extreme silence that weighed on their motionless heads. Only the eyes were not afraid and rested coldly on Milienne. She refused to attend the funeral service and insisted she be kissed on the cheek by all the strangers. When they left with the Old Man, she stayed behind on the doorstep, her great body like a dried husk against the banister. Only once the car's motor had started did she begin running in their direction (pieces of silver had come out of her apron and rolled into the dust where, seen from a certain angle, they shone brightly.) "Come on, we've got to go," Milien said. "Just act as if you don't see her." Milienne was hitting the glass with her fists with all her might. She only wanted to say something everyone knew and no one wanted to hear. The Old Man lowered the window and Milienne stuck her head through (those black spots on her face, sea gulls held back with elastic, and that red nose and especially the dentures, the false tarnished teeth, the white tongue). She said: "Do you know, it's not his house. It's my house." And she burst out laughing, which was like a shower of scorching slaps upon his face. "Get off," said the Old Man. With his hand he hit the fingers that were holding onto the door. Milienne gritted her teeth, grimaced, and then, when she opened her mouth, there was such an outburst that the Old Man lost his temper; he pushed the door with all his might and slipped out (like a big cat jumping into a flowery hedge), and lifted his leg; his foot disappeared somewhere under the dress while Milienne began howling, rolling in the dust, shaking spasmodically with raging arms. "Couldn't you take her into the house?" said the Old Man to his grandsons who had stepped out of the car. Four people were needed to take hold of Milienne and lay her down in the bedroom in the double bed. He looked on from the doorway, full of hate for her; he was so small that it was only through stubbornness that he could overcome her; that he could break her to remake her more in his own image. Thus he still needed to learn patience because kicking her was only cowardly. He was well aware that he'd been caught in a trap, as if they'd wanted to take his old age from him. (Yet, being idle, yawning, reading a few pages from the Holy Book, rocking yourself for hours, looking at T.V. after supper till your eyes watered, petting the cats, wasn't all that nothing and worthy only of insults?) Some days he went almost crazy because he couldn't stand the idea that he would never be left alone; someone would always take him away from himself. Sometimes he had such selfish needs. Nothing was important except what went on in himself. When he had one of those days, Milien didn't say a word; he sat in the armchair before the window, stared at the tree tops, pulled at his pipe and thought of diseases, of the sun, of the pumpkins that were coming up fine in the field behind the house, and the rumps of big animals, and noisy parties where he was always the clown, disguised as the bogeyman for the children surrounding him in fiendish circles. What would he have done with his false Milienne in the whirlwind of his imagination? The truth was that they had never had anything to say to each other. They were strangers to each other, horse traders caught in the rules of a game they'd invented and which they would not get out of except through death. (Nothing must be forgotten, despite the haste. And certainly not Milienne's underclothes which he thought of sometimes after reading the paper. He read slowly, spelling the words and moving his lips, bent over the sheets with his big back rounded, and the pages, the big pages moving before his eyes. He'd have a lot to say about this paper, for Milien had a good memory for things he read. Few images slipped past him and what he didn't understand, remained on the surface of his being and escaped him in feverish moments; then it took on its whole meaning and drove him into holy rages to Milienne's confusion. She was incapable of freeing herself from the spell of this terrifying voice other than by breaking a dish or remembering the elephants coupling in songs) — SO, there was, as has already been said, Milienne's underclothes which he thought of sometimes after reading the newspaper (it took him a week to read the Monday paper), then he moved the armchair, stretched out and let his head rest on the leatherette back-rest. He then took his hand from his pocket and put his fingers under his nose: he liked to smell the musky odors of the body's secret places; there was something almost tender in them that softened him and allowed him a certain tranquility; he then crossed his legs and let himself go into his dream and had false memories of Milienne. But that wasn't what mattered, for just as she was, in her hugeness and fat, she appeared desirable to him, good to lick and easy to bruise. He sucked the flesh on her arms and all that was big in Milienne swelled up with a new life, destroying the myth of this false exist-ence that he lived with a dry, unaffectionate, authoritative woman who hated men and obscenity. At first, Milien used to get mad: this woman who refused him everything; why was she so mean that she even in-vaded his dreams? She wore impossible underwear; that's what he felt like talking about. When, in an angry moment, he lifted her dress over her head to see her bum (which he knew was beautiful because he had seen it once through a half-open door and was so floored by those heavy white buttocks that he was on the point of opening the door completely and jumping on his woman, throwing her onto the bed and biting into that warm milky stuff), it remained absolutely forbidden to him. Milienne was wearing long beige underpants that nullified her sex and matted the crack between her thighs as if she had already died there and could no longer be touched, except with decay. Or else he still had to recreate this woman, to make her similar to what he wanted her to be because he loved her and loved himself through what she was. It wasn't for nothing that he had recourse so much to his ancient mythologies, to Rang Rallonge, to his land, to stone partitions in the fields, to Milienne helping him with the hay. (She got into the cart and took hold of the reins; she was a big hard-working queen, hard to knock the breath out of, with a man's muscles and an endurance which he himself never showed except in fits of anger. Her breasts were free under her dress and moved when the cart jolted. Milien held the reins with one hand and placed his fingers in his crotch, happy to be beside Milienne who was clucking her tongue. And the brown gobs of chewed tobacco splattered like wingless gadflies against the rocks. There remained only to speak of the stallion, snorting and grinding his teeth on the bit that cut his mouth. "Believe me, Milienne, I assure you that I love you, Milienne darling.") He had never said that. What was happening did not have to end with words. Words added nothing and were a threat because they could only be arbitrary, said in such a way that confusion remained always possible and even desirable, so that the illusions, sustained for years in an unshakable solitude, would not break and leave the body and soul naked and suddenly vulnerable and ugly. Understanding that was not easy; you could never be distracted and you would have to live your everyday life in a kind of illumination which Milienne was totally incapable of in her illness. With this pain nesting in her stomach, she had become capricious and hostile and jealous of the effortlessness of Milien's gestures. He was, seated in his chair, a kind of provocation: that pink sleeping flesh, those old lines, so old that you would have thought they were infantile (there was so much ingenuity in the creases and a kind of careless delicacy), those folkloric songs and religious hymns he hummed with his lips, juggling the consonants; it all told her that she would die soon and that death would have no one but her. After her

death, another Milienne would take her place in the house and undo what she had begun to accomplish and had not the time to finish. That's to say, she would force Milien to be born again, to leave his old worn skin and come into a new world, hers, which she had patiently and painstakingly constructed since childhood. (He was a poor old man lost in false memories, inventing stormy rivers in the back of his head, and cows, cart wheels, wild stallions, children he could never have conceived in his sterility, great assemblies of men and women in enormous villages and unending parties at the center of which he stood like a holy patriarch: calm, completely calm — and just. He had read Mathilde's Bible too much, too many angels had appeared, announcing that for having waited to talk so much, he must be silent and live only his inner life amid the everyday dream and the cats jumping onto his knees for long caresses. When she would reach the point of death and Milien would be bent over her, looking into her eyes but not seeing her because deep down he had always denied her existence, then, with a thousand exorcising repetitions, she would find nothing more biting to say than: "I hate you, Milien. How I hate you, Milien." . . . .
. . . .
. . . .

. . . . He was walking through pools of water. All kinds of sounds were ringing in his ears. He was moving through the dark, shivering, stumbling against stones, his teeth chattering. He had lost his hat and his wet pants stuck to his legs. His eyes were drowning, soon they would sink and leave him defenseless against the monsters coming out of the shadows and jumping into the landscape. All the hideous creatures he had repressed within himself were rising to his eyes, obstructing them with their bloody battles: he now saw only pig's entrails slashed up inside the jaws of dogs, calves with ripped open stomachs, demented bulls with cut legs, copulating in those stomachs where the calves were rotting, rolled up in a ball — and cats strangled and drying on small beams; obese women lamenting because of the umbilical cords caught in their vaginas; crippled children lying in boxes with their tongues hanging out of their mouths and little penises like horns below their stomachs; and ramshackle houses (he was right in front of the house of his youth, the one he had lived in with his first Milienne and built with his own hands with tenacity and love; and had had to sell when death treacherously seized his woman before the vats with bones boiling inside). He no longer remembered exactly how it had happened: no doubt he had drunk too much, or had cried too much, or had been too calm. Let's just say that one morning, coming back dead tired from all the ploughing, he was no longer in the same house and did not recognize his wife, the new Milienne, who was lying in bed, groaning and holding her swollen stomach that looked as if she were going to give birth to an enormous monstrous beast. Everything had come from this misunderstanding; he had pushed open one door too many and his head rolled to the floor. Suddenly, seeing the false Milienne dying in the bedroom, he lost everything: from now on he would have to tell himself stories, recreate the past, marry another Milienne and live in an unfriendly house to atone and so that the authentic memories might inhabit him again, filling his new head with simple reassuring images. In her agony, Milienne was alone, hideous and thin. Her stomach was opening; it was steaming hot, dirty, giving off a horrible stink. Milien took out his handkerchief and held it to his nose. He was thinking of the one obscene gesture Milienne had made toward him. One night while he was sound asleep, she slid up against him, covering his whole body with hers; she drew out her tongue and pushed it into his nose and began moving it slowly, sliding it in and out like a short penis. That excited

him so much that he ejaculated hard somewhere between her naked thighs. Then he
sneezed and smeared Milienne's cheeks
with snot. She was looking at him, smiling
with her small evil eyes, swallowing the
snot, completely crazy. Her heart beat fast
in her breast and she was talking wildly;
she squeezed her legs together, rubbed her
wet pubis against his body with passion-
ate fury that was like no other and could
only end with her death. He could not
free himself from that dream: Milienne
could rant as much as she liked, beat her
head against the bed's steel posts and call
for help because she was losing too much
blood, he didn't hear her; he saw in her
only that impure act and its long expiation
in horrible suffering. He would have hit her
rather than bring assistance; he would have
hurt her for hysteria was invading the room
and soon would prove unbearable. Everything was becoming hazy, shapes did a
danse macabre before his eyes. He could
no longer control himself. There was Milienne's lifeless body on the floor, fat and
provocative with evil life; he lost his head,
gripped the cane with his two hands, made
one step, his body sore from having held
onto the stallion bucking in its harness,
its mouth bloody. He began to hit her. The
cane was the specter of justice beating the
stiff white body — yes, that's what it was.

Ramshackle houses moved through the night, disintegrating into the shadows, retreating into the frightening back country populated by men who were monsters playing evil tricks on the animals. (He had sat down on the steps, the sign *Funeral Parlor* was a swarm of motionless butterflies in the air, a violet glass eye that hypnotized him. It was in this house that Milienne had died; there her body had been exposed, surrounded by funeral wreaths. After the burial, he would not see his children again, nor the land he had sold to pay for the funeral, nor the possessions he had patiently accumulated. So he had sat down on the steps and had cried, lost in a heavy dream. His old friend, Chien Chien Pichlotte, must have lowered the window-blind to undress in the dark; he saw him smearing his skin with dry shit, his lips were a sun at the bottom of his face; and he was on all fours on the floor, barking, an old dog used up by long illness.) Milien remained staring a long time at the *Funeral Parlor* sign. The F no longer lit up, everything disintegrated into the inarticulate. This was about the moment when the Old Man got up. He would go look for his watch, forgotten in the cemetery; then, that done, he would have to notify the doctor that Milienne was leaving . . . .
. . . .

148

. . . . .He did not have
to lift the knocker, for the door opened as
soon as he had walked up the steps; the
doctor was there with his black bag in his
hand, dressed in a hard hat and an old
beige raincoat whose sleeves were shiny
from too much use. "Things going no
better, eh?" he said, giving his arm to Milien. The two men made their way down the
walk. The steel taps on the heels of the
doctor's shoes began clicking against the
stones. It was calming to walk this way in
the dark, shoulder to shoulder, arm in arm,
like old acquaintances. "Cigarette?" said
the doctor. The Old Man began to laugh
to accentuate the complicity between
himself and his companion. "Are we going
to harness up the stallion?" said Milien.
"No need to," said the doctor. The rain
had stopped falling, the worms must be
shining in the grass. The asphalt was a
skating rink; could Saint-Jean-de-Dieu be
anything other than an egg-yolk thrown in
the air? "Let's stop," said Milien. He did
not want to arrive too fast: to give Milienne
all the odds would have been a mistake;
there was no need to be too loyal and let
oneself be carried away by sentiment.
"You'll have to take the pills I'm giving
you," said the doctor, looking him in the
eyes with neither anger nor friendship, as
if he were talking in the void to someone

149

who was no longer there. The Old Man laughed again. His large shoulders were shaking. "My God," he said, "we can start again." The walk resumed. The doctor pushed open the gate, the house was enormous at the end of the yard. The doctor threw his cigarette on the sidewalk and snuffed it out under his foot. Everything was unfolding in slow-motion, gestures were being enlarged. They were made with indecision, as if the event had to be stalled, not to rush or anticipate what was going to happen. An infinity passed between the moment the doctor removed his foot from the cigarette butt and the one when he made the three ritual steps toward the staircase. Interminable words were spoken in a hushed voice. The Old Man no longer stopped talking; meaningless and without any order, the words pushed against each other in his mouth in a final attempt to voice what was still nameless. "Hurry up," said the doctor. "Not right away," the Old Man groaned. "Not right away, eh?" (The starved cats must be wandering through the dirty deserted house; a thick coating of dust covered everything with an absence that would not settle; the sink was rusty; along the cupboard doors, spiders had woven huge webs. The two men were about to stumble against the useless past; they were about to drown in heavy despair in the refuse of seventy-five years of existence. Behind the door you could hear the cats clawing the furniture and their distressed meowing. They must have grown much thinner, skins hanging awkwardly on bones that were jutting out. The Old Man had said "ah!" and he fell on the doorstep into the dog shit. He was groaning with his mouth open, his only tooth like an ivory uvula before the palace. (His body was turning round somewhere in a whirlpool in the Boisbouscache, blue and swollen like a goatskin, an old blue baby who was going to split open and pollute the river's water, opening the country to the plague, tumors and leprosy. Bodies would become factory chimneys, alchemical formulas breaking ancient fertile worlds. Everything would end in depigmentation and decrease. The Boisbouscache water was being dirtied with blood and excrement and he himself could not stop turning and twisting in the whirl-pool, crowned with a hat of foam. Leeches were gluing themselves to his stomach, sucking what remained of the false life in his navel. He wanted to scream to stop this sorcery but he no longer had a mouth, nor eyes; only his nose remained to be eaten by the electric eels zigzagging against the waves.) "Come, come," said the doctor. He had opened his bag and listened to the Old Man's heart after unbuttoning his shirt.

He pinched the burning cheeks and looked into the white eye sheltered behind the eyelids. (He would not come back, he was too full of water and had lost too much blood. He was drawing away too quickly from his memories. The boxes were going adrift in the water, floating and knocking against the wreckage. Ridiculous and inhuman, everything would end in the river.) The doctor was massaging his heart, mumbling soothing words which he could not hear well since they reached him distorted and undecipherable. "Milienne," he could have added. And: "It's for Milienne, doctor, for Milienne." The Old Man was heavy in his arms and there was now a strong smell of urine which made him sneeze. He was able to move the doorknob; the hinges grated. Scores of big yellow cats dashed through the opening, jumped the fence and were lost in the fields. He touched the switch and the house lit up. He could hardly breathe for the stink. The floor creaked, it was covered with refuse. The sofa springs were steel spirals, everything was dying; the house was a trap, a decaying force in which the Old Man would soon be lost amid tears and sobs. "Calm down," said the doctor. It was suddenly cold, the house now a refrigerator gone out of whack, making the rusty floor nails snap. (Green mushrooms covered the heaps of refuse in menacing islands.) He was still holding the Old Man in his arms and did not dare to put him down anywhere, for he feared that he would become like this sordid filthy place; he would be swallowed up in a decomposition whose only goal was the proliferation of parasites now awakening in the dark to swarm over the motionless body, bloat it with grey tumors that would give off overwhelming smells. He pushed open the bedroom door with his foot and pulled the string to turn on the light; he was as if beside himself, moving through a silence that forced him to make gestures he knew were ridiculous, having tried them too many times. (It was this small child he was carrying to the bed, a cripple whose artificial limb was the color of his old flesh — it resembled a crab's pincer. He was weary: why didn't the Old Man die? He was standing before the window, the man's body in his arms, and he wasn't crying, for all this left him indifferent. Finally he no longer even smelled the odors. His only hope was that he would soon be rid of the Old Man.) He laid him down on the bed and took off his boots; the feet were cold. He massaged them slowly, giving them the warmth from his hands with care. The Old Man had started trembling again. (Could this have happened long after his Milienne's death?

He could no longer leave the house; his tooth was becoming cold now that a cavity was boring through the enamel. Sometimes, placing the tip of his tongue on the hole, he sucked up a bit of pus and swallowed it. He had never tasted anything like that before; it was sweet and sour at the same time, making him shiver. His whole mouth was like a gong; he had to hold onto the furniture not to fall into the traps that were opening in the floor. He had pulled open the cupboard door, his fingertips were feeling the dusty cans, the empty bottles, the rotten onions; he was cursing and swearing, a great rage having risen within him and destroyed his serenity; he was as if in a muddy pool, his huge body moving and rocking like a pendulum. Finally he found the pliers he was looking for; for a moment his head was silent, as if cut off from the noisy serpents that were making their way through his stomach. He came back into the room and lit the big lamp on the dresser. He looked at himself in the old mirror whose silver had come off in places, and he became aware that large pieces of his body were eaten up in the glass. He opened his mouth; the tooth was there, behind his lips, yellow and provoking. He opened the pliers. His hand trembled, he was crying, unable to put the instrument into his mouth. When his tongue touched the steel, he shook violently and shut his eyes. The moon had just gone under somewhere in the Boisbouscache. The sky was flattening down over the houses that were like matchboxes glowing in the night. He was howling, salivating, the pliers jammed round the unshakable tooth. The enamel crumbled and he spat out pieces, scowling. "No," he said, "no. Oh no." He dropped the pliers on the floor between his legs which had never seemed so long to him. Soon it would be too hot and he would lose consciousness in the smoke, in the obscure, senseless world. He knelt down again before the cupboard. He no longer saw anything but his tooth, it took up the whole space of his eyes; he suffered inside, his whole body being torn with pain. The tooth would be transformed into a coffin in which he would end his days, sucking his thumb. He unwound the fishing line, testing its sureness with his fists. (The red marks on his palms. The blood bubbling out of the cut wart.) Then he fastened his tooth, took a hundred steps in the gloomy kitchen with the cats rubbing against his legs. Everything was becoming distorted like a zebra skin; there were pockets of sweat and spots in his eyes. He knotted the end of the string to the doorknob. To be tied to things didn't calm him at all. The images were like a whirlwind in his head; they came out of his mouth, eyes and ears, cracking the walls. They were luminous rockets burrowing holes in the night. He held his breath and took two steps back, sounding the line. Now everything would take only an instant. He closed his eyes and kicked the door hard with his foot. And his whole body came out of him and was spread bloodily on the dirty floor. He no longer had a jaw, he was drowning in pus. His tooth at the end of the string was an impossibility.) The doctor poured hot water into the basin. He had taken some towels and washed the Old Man whom he had just undressed. The motionless body on the bed was a threat against which he could not defend himself, except by talking. What he was saying no longer mattered; the Old Man had already gone beyond words a long time ago, holding onto the taut cord of silence in the egotistical suffering that would never permit itself to be touched again. The most he could do would be to allow him to die alone. "The pills," he said, "don't forget the pills." He put the stethoscope back into the bag along with the tiny flashlight. He pulled down the blind. "Sleep. You must sleep a lot now." He took his hat. The Old Man's eyes were cat's eyes that would never leave him again. He was anxious to leave the house now: so much hypocrisy sickened him. The Old Man lifted his hand, but did not say anything. "Try to spend a good night," said the doctor. And he left this way, after pulling the covers over the Old Man and snuffing out the lamp. The Old Man heard the door slam. He straightened up a little and looked into the night, maddened because his eyes would not adjust to the dark. The bed, swallowed up by the darkness, was rolling down into the bowels of the earth where everything would be warm at last, noble and endless and without indecision. He let his head fall back to the pillow; the black mass could begin now that the night was full and the devils were coming up from the cellar and between the walls, their powerful tails like noisy whips and their forks red with hell-fire, piercing hard into the flesh, tearing apart his body as it twisted on the bed. He would fall to the floor and be a bloody wound, rotten meat that the devils would tear apart in great hunks and eat, seated in a circle around him. Heart, liver and stommach, all were given over to the devils for their rejoicing. He heard angels' wings beating above the black mass. He saw the curly heads of the cherubim, the golden noses, the motionless eyes and the smiling lips. He heard the sacred songs, the exorcising incantations; everything tasted of burnt flesh and blood boiling in the veins.

He was sweating, his head empty of all images; he was full of holes. Nothing now could be withheld, observed, accepted or refused. He would belong from now on only to what was descending, pushing down, disappearing, losing itself in the company of the devils with the wicked eyes. There remained only one final thought to be expressed which would take form only on the other side of the mirror, in the white motionless country ....
....
....
....
....
......(November 14 1970/February 3 1971)

Printed by
Les Éditions Marquis Ltée
Montmagny